WAIT FOR ME

WAIT FOR ME

NATASHA WILLIAMS

For my sons, who give me the courage to
do almost anything.

ACKNOWLEDGEMENTS

My heartfelt thanks goes to Dhashika Ramgolam, who has been so helpful and supportive, and instrumental in making my dream a reality.

Special thanks to Laa'iqah Domingo for indulging me, understanding my infatuation, and for encouraging me to soldier on.

Nicole Williams – the inspiration behind Harlow – thank you for taking my imagination to places it would never have gone without you.

I am especially thankful to my sons, Romano, Ricardo and Reilly, for enduring my absence during the writing process and for being patient with me while I worked.

And to my beautiful mom...thank you so much for everything, always.

PROLOGUE

Johannesburg, South Africa

Six years ago

Shelby stared at the phone in her hand. "Another one bites the dust," she mumbled as she leaned back into the headrest. A moment later, her phone rang. "Hello?" she answered as if she didn't know who it was.

"Are you just going to sit outside in your car all night?" Harlow asked. "You know I can see you, right?"

Shelby looked at Harlow's house and noticed her peering through the curtain of her living room window. She waved. "I just broke up with Tyler," she said.

"Why?"

"Because I have to take the boys to their soccer matches tomorrow and he says they're too old to rely on me this much."

"But you're a single mom," Harlow said incredulously. "They might be teenagers, but you're all they have."

"Yep."

"Did you invite him to join you?"

"It crossed my mind. But I don't want the kids to know about him...in case he decides to disappear," Shelby said with a shrug.

"Are you coming in?" asked Harlow.

She watched as Harlow moved away from the window. "On my way."

The delicious smell of popcorn invaded her nostrils the moment she stepped through the door. It was warm and inviting and her mood instantly perked up. Movie night

1

with Harlow was something she looked forward to. It was only three nights a year, but it was the only time she got to be a person, not just a mother.

"Are you okay?" Harlow asked when Shelby joined her in the kitchen.

"I'm fine. It wasn't really working out anyway. He was too demanding of my time."

Harlow shook her head. "You're raising three children on your own. How much time does he think you have available?"

"I don't know, but at least I don't have to make excuses anymore," Shelby said as she put the kettle on to boil and started making hot chocolate. "What are we watching tonight?" she asked, changing the subject.

"Ultimate Combatants marathon! All of them!" Harlow said excitedly.

Shelby's jaw dropped. "But that's eight movies!" she said, picturing her own DVD collection of the renowned Second World War action movie franchise in her cabinet back home.

"Maybe we can make it a weekend event instead of just one night?" Harlow asked, lifting her shoulders hopefully. "The boys can join us."

Shelby laughed. "I'll see what I can do."

A cold front had hit the country and it was one of the coldest nights of the year. A howling wind rattled the windows and although a gas heater warmed the room, Shelby pulled a shaggy blanket over her shoulders.

"What do you think about Garridan Luca?" she asked.

"Who?" Harlow asked, looking at Shelby as she sipped her hot chocolate.

"The actor who plays Sergeant Jameson," Shelby said, pointing to the TV where the hero's intense blue eyes focused in on his target over the barrel of the rifle he wielded.

"Jameson's cute. But I'm more of a Müller fan," said Harlow, smiling as the attractive villain fought his way through a barrage of soldiers.

"I think Garridan's gorgeous and an amazing actor. I love all the roles he's played."

"Roles?" Harlow asked with raised eyebrows.

"He acts in more than just these movies, you know?"

"He's *your* crush, Shel. I only remember him from those soapies my mom used to watch long ago," Harlow said, turning her attention back to the TV.

Shelby shrugged, but it was soon replaced with a swoon as they watched one of her favourite scenes in the movie involving Sergeant Jameson's love interest. "Just look at that. When last did a man stand when you entered a room?"

"Never," Harlow sniggered. "Don't you just love how he says 'ma'am' when he greets her?"

"I wish I could meet a man like Jameson. Brave, loyal. And just look at how longingly he gazes at her," Shelby said dreamily.

Harlow sighed.

"I think I was born in the wrong era," said Shelby. "I don't know anyone as chivalrous as these men."

"Chivalry died long ago, my cousin," said Harlow,

chewing on some popcorn. "I'm so tired of being disappointed or hurt."

"Maybe we should do something about it."

Harlow paused the movie and turned to face Shelby. "Like what?"

"We could go away? Visit another country? I want to experience something new."

"Spain," Harlow said, her dark brown eyes lighting up. "No, Cuba!"

"How about the Caribbean Islands?"

"Beach vacations are where people meet their soulmate!" Harlow cried and Shelby could almost see the romantic fantasies budding in her cousin's mind.

"I'd have to wait until the boys are older," said Shelby. "We'd need at least a month for a trip halfway across the world and I can't imagine saddling anyone with my responsibilities for that long."

Harlow's eyes widened. "We can do it for my thirtieth. Something positive to look forward to as I usher in a new decade!" she said excitedly.

"Six more years," Shelby sighed. "Turning thirty might be exciting, but forty-two is hardly something to look forward to."

"Isn't forty-two the new thirty? Come on, it'll be fun. And we'll have enough time to work everything out."

"Okay," Shelby smiled. "Let's do it. We should start planning it soon."

"I think this will work. The Wilson girls off to distant lands on a great adventure," Harlow said, nodding slowly.

"And meeting the men of their dreams," she added, clicking the remote control to resume the movie.

"I think I'll give the dream guy fantasy a skip. I'm never dating anyone ever again. Period," said Shelby. "I'm just going to pretend Sergeant Jameson's my boyfriend. Men these days are clueless when it comes to women."

"Can you believe we're finally here, Shel?" Harlow asked when they exited the taxi.

"It feels like a dream," said Shelby, taking in the city around her.

She was a ball of nerves and excitement. She and Harlow had planned this trip for so long, it was surreal finally standing in the street they'd picked out on the internet and marked off on a map years before.

"It's as if everything we've ever wanted has finally been given to us. As if we dreamt it into existence," Harlow said as they crossed the busy road.

"That's profound," said Shelby, pondering the words. "It really is everything we've hoped it would be."

"The only thing that would make it better is finally meeting my dream guy. Imagine just running into a handsome stranger and hitting it off." Harlow had a dreamy, faraway look in her eye as she twirled a strand of hair around her finger.

"You're such a romantic," Shelby laughed. "Things like that only happen in movies and we all know those stories are made up by people like you who believe in happily ever after."

Harlow rolled her eyes. "You really need to have more faith. You never know what surprises life could bring you."

Shelby could only shake her head at her cousin. They'd been in Miami for only a day and Harlow was already in love with the city and the promises it held. Magic City. Right in line with her love for all things fantasy and mystical.

"Not interested," Shelby said. "I'm here to fulfil some of my dreams and meeting a man isn't one of them."

For years they'd dreamt about this trip, starting with a tour of the Caribbean Islands and ending with an Independence Day celebration. It was a long and difficult road to get there. Years of planning and saving, which was almost derailed by challenges life threw at them. But they persevered. It was a phenomenal journey, and well worth it.

With Miami being the final leg of their month-long trip, Shelby looked forward to taking it all in. As much as she loved learning about the Islands' histories and rich culture, and meeting some of the most incredible people, she was glad to finally be in a place that felt more like home.

They spent the afternoon trying to locate the different sights they'd planned on seeing. They'd done the research and prepared their itinerary, but finding their way around was more challenging than they expected it to be. Eventually, they gave up their touristy approach and just explored. There was so much to see and they thoroughly enjoyed recognising some of the buildings and landmarks they'd seen in movies and read about in books.

Towards the end of their day's exploration, they decided to get a drink before returning to their rental home.

"I saw a place not far from here," Harlow said, pointing to a row of restaurants and coffee shops close by.

On the way there, Shelby noticed a beautiful hat as they passed one of the street vendors. "Hold on," she said, removing the colourful, wide-brimmed straw hat from the stand. "Isn't this gorgeous?"

Harlow nodded. "It's very sophisticated. Try it on."

Shelby placed the hat on her head. "Look at me," she said in a French accent. "Je m'appelle Shelby."

GARRIDAN

Garridan walked towards his car. He and Marc were discussing their thoughts on the meeting they'd just attended, and Quincy followed closely behind them. Marc pointed out a building he'd mentioned earlier and when Garridan looked up, he spotted her across the busy street. He stopped in his tracks.

She stood in front of a sidewalk vending stall trying on a colourful hat, smiling brightly at the woman to her side who held up a phone to take a picture. The one with the hat pouted and flirted with the camera as she tossed her head back, the tips of her long, curly brown hair reaching for her thighs. Her friend laughed in response.

After she placed the hat back on the stand, she peered over her friend's shoulder to look at the photo and her face lit up when she laughed at what she saw. They chatted animatedly as they walked away from the stall. She looked so happy, Garridan wished he could hear what she was saying over the bustle of the traffic between them. He gestured for his friends to follow him before he quickly dashed across the road, veering between oncoming cars as he ran towards the stall.

"How much?" he asked the vendor.

"Ten dollars."

Garridan drew a twenty dollar note from his pocket and tossed it to the vendor. "Thanks. Keep the change!" he shouted as he rushed to catch up with the women.

They were at an intersection. The traffic light had just turned red and they stood in silence as they waited to cross. Garridan approached them tentatively, simultaneously wondering what he'd say to her and taking in her appearance. Her light blue skinny jeans hugged the gentle curve of her hips and thighs, and the black halterneck top showed off her soft femininity. Luxurious hair cascaded down her back. When he reached her, he noticed just how petite she was. The top of her head reaching just below his shoulder.

He cleared his throat. "Excuse me," he said, tapping her shoulder.

She gasped and spun around to face him. He wished he could see her eyes, but they were hidden behind dark sunglasses.

"I'm sorry. I didn't mean to startle you," he said, holding up his hands apologetically.

She exhaled slowly. "It's fine. No worries," she said with a smile and Garridan noticed an accent.

The light turned green, but none of them moved to cross. She looked at Garridan expectantly as the other pedestrians walked past and around them.

He held the hat out towards her. "I saw you at the stall. You look beautiful with this on and I think you should have it."

She took it hesitantly and her smile widened. "Thanks so much. That's really sweet of you." Her cheeks turned a flattering shade of pink.

"Are you from around here?" he asked.

"No. We're on vacation from South Africa," she replied, pointing between her and her friend.

"In that case, welcome to the USA!" he said brightly, opening his arms dramatically.

The women laughed at his theatrics.

"I'm Garridan." He held his hand out to her.

"I'm Shelby," she said, shaking his hand. "This is my cousin, Harlow."

He shook Harlow's hand and turned around. "This is Marc, and Quincy," he said, indicating to his friends.

They exchanged pleasant greetings, but an awkward silence soon fell over them as Garridan stared wordlessly at Shelby. She shifted uncomfortably.

"How long are you here for?" he asked. "I'd like to take you out sometime if possible. Perhaps show you around?"

Harlow gaped and nudged Shelby with her elbow, and Garridan watched with amusement as Shelby ignored her cousin's reaction.

"I'd like that," Shelby said. "We're here for Independence Day and our flight back home is on the sixth."

"So I have five days to choose from?" Garridan asked.

"We do have plans for some of those days," Harlow interjected.

At the same time, Marc stepped forward to whisper into Garridan's ear.

"Give me your number and we'll figure it out," Garridan said, handing his phone to Shelby. "I wish I didn't have to, but I gotta leave now."

After punching in her number, she handed his phone to him. "It's saved as Shelby SA."

"Thank you," he smiled. "I'll call you later if that's okay."

Shelby cradled the hat to her chest and nodded.

They exchanged goodbyes and the ladies crossed the road. And as the guys headed back to their car, Garridan turned to catch one last glimpse of her, but she'd already disappeared into the crowd.

"Did you even hear a word I said?" Harlow asked irritably.

Shelby sat staring at nothing. After their encounter with Garridan, she spent the rest of the day in a daze. They'd returned to their rental house and were sitting on the living room floor eating burgers while planning their outing for the next day. But she couldn't focus, her mind kept drifting to him.

"Sorry, Harlow. But I'm still in shock."

Harlow snickered. "I don't blame you. I can't believe you're actually living my dream!" she laughed, shaking her head. "The handsome stranger."

"But is he really a stranger?" asked Shelby.

"What do you mean?"

"It's him," Shelby said, handing her phone to Harlow.

Harlow looked at the picture on the screen and frowned. "Please don't tell me you're still using your fake movie boyfriend to repel guys."

"I'm not using him for anything," Shelby grumbled. "He's Sergeant Jameson from the war movies, remember?"

"As if I could forget Jameson," Harlow said sarcastically.

Shelby sighed. "The Garridan we met today *is* Garridan Luca who plays Jameson."

She watched as her cousin's eyes bugged out.

"How did I not notice?" Harlow said, sputtering as she

choked on her drink. "But in my defence, he looks different. Older."

"Well, it has been about fifteen years since he acted in those movies. I think he still looks amazing."

"Wow!" Harlow said. "So you're actually going on a date with your celeb crush?" she mused as the realisation finally started sinking in. "This is a huge deal."

"Do you think he'll call?" Shelby asked, afraid to sound too gullible.

Harlow shrugged. "Honestly? I don't know. If *normal* guys disappoint us all the time, who knows what famous men are capable of. I'd be surprised if he actually did call."

"We'll have to wait and see," Shelby said.

"I love how he just walked up to you and asked you out."

"I nearly passed out when I turned around and saw him." Shelby giggled as she recalled her reaction at the time.

"Confidence is a very admirable trait," Harlow said. "And he didn't try stupid pick-up lines or flattery. He just asked."

"Maybe that's how celebrities do things. I guess they're just more confident than other men."

"He's even more attractive in person," Harlow said, looking at the picture again. "But why didn't you say anything when he introduced himself?"

Shelby shrugged. "I didn't want to put him off. I don't think celebrities actually enjoy people fawning over them. Remember how much I hate attention? I can imagine it must be much worse for famous people."

"You're probably right. But will you tell him eventually? Or are you going to pretend you never knew about him?"

"I'm not sure. I don't want to come across as just another fan." Shelby cringed at the word. "But I also don't want him to think I don't appreciate his craft or admire his talent."

"I think you're going to have to figure that out soon," Harlow said, handing the phone back to Shelby. "Because lover boy just sent you a message."

Shelby took the phone and a sudden chill rippled through her body. Her heartbeat spiked as she read the message on the screen: *Hi, Shelby. It's Garridan.* With trembling fingers, she replied.

Garridan was easy-going and Shelby felt comfortable speaking to him. But soon after they sent their initial string of text messages, he called her because he preferred calls to texts. The sound of his voice triggered a whirlwind of emotions. Shelby worked hard to play it cool as they got to know each other, but she was overwhelmed. Never in her wildest dreams did she think it was possible. That she'd be speaking to him on the phone.

When their conversation turned to their date, she panicked. She hadn't been out with a man in years and she wasn't sure she'd be able to pull off her composed performance in person.

"I can't wait to see you," he said. "What would you like to do?"

"I'd like to go somewhere we can talk," she replied, uncertain about being so specific.

"Sure. I'll text you the details."

After the call, Harlow returned to the room. "I haven't seen you blush so many times in one day," she smirked.

"It's so overwhelming, Harlow," Shelby defended herself, embarrassed for acting like a lovesick schoolgirl.

"It's okay to feel that way, Shel. I'm so excited for you."

"You don't think I'm being stupid for doing this?"

"Never! Do you have any idea how many people would *kill* to be you right now? You're so lucky!"

Shelby held her arm out towards Harlow, who scrunched her eyebrows in confusion.

"What?" Harlow asked.

"Pinch me."

"Why?"

Shelby flopped dramatically onto the couch and gushed, "I can't believe I'm actually going on a date with Garridan Luca!"

"Breathe", Harlow said as she leaned over Shelby, fanning her face with a tissue. "Breathe," she giggled.

Shelby lay curled on the bed, hyperventilating. She couldn't believe Harlow was enjoying her torment. She peeked at her through one eye. "I'm glad you find this amusing."

This sent Harlow into a fit of laughter. "It's only a date and you're acting like you're about to walk down the aisle."

"It's only my first date in a very long time. I really like him and I seriously don't want to mess this up."

"Relax, Shel. You've been speaking to him for the past two days and he hasn't ghosted you yet. Stop overthinking things. You look pale and sickly, and he'll be here in fifteen minutes." Harlow tugged on Shelby's arm coaxing her up from the bed. "Here, let me fix your hair."

They'd woken up early to prepare Shelby for her date with Garridan. He withheld details, but asked her to wear comfortable clothes and to pack a bathing suit. The fact that they were going to the beach was daunting enough, but it was Harlow's insistence that she *shave all over because tonight might be the first night of the rest of your life* that sent Shelby into a flat panic.

"I wish I told him I don't like surprises," she complained.

"No, you're a control freak, and I like that someone is

trying to surprise you and wants you to feel special. Just enjoy it."

Shelby looked at her reflection in the mirror. She'd never felt that nervous before and hoped Garridan would forgive her if she stammered and blundered her way through the day.

"What's going on, Shel?" Harlow asked, crossing her arms as she leaned against the wall beside her. "You're usually so confident. I've never seen you this flustered before."

"I guess it's because this is all so unexpected. It's easy to be confident around a normal man, but Garridan is nothing like the men we're used to. I don't even know why he's interested in me." Shelby paused and took a deep breath. "Also, I've liked him for so long, it feels like he's been in my life forever. I'd be really disappointed if he didn't like me too."

"You look pretty and you're a fun, intelligent woman," Harlow continued her pep talk. "He already likes you. All you have to do is be yourself so he can fall in love with you."

"I doubt that will happen, but I'll try. Thank you." She took another deep breath and sent up a silent prayer that everything would be alright.

When the doorbell chimed, Harlow left to let Garridan in while Shelby threw some last-minute essentials into her bag. A few minutes later, she left her room and followed the sound of Harlow and Garridan's hushed conversation. Her breath caught as her gaze fell on him when she entered the living room where they were standing. He wore a black short-sleeved shirt and dark blue jeans, his beard was fuller than it was when they first met, and his dark hair was stylishly tousled. He looked like he just stepped off a page of a fashion magazine.

He stopped mid-sentence when she approached them and flashed a gorgeous smile that made her knees weak and her heart skip several beats.

GARRIDAN

arridan held out his arms and Shelby stepped into his embrace. He greeted her with a gentle kiss on her cheek. "Hi," he whispered.

"Hi," she said as she took a step back.

She smelled amazing. Like shampoo and shower gel and perfume. The combination of fragrances wreaked havoc on his senses. She looked more than amazing in a flirty floral dress and a denim jacket that was rolled up once at the sleeves. Beaded jewellery adorned her arms. The outfit was completed by the hat he gave her and a studious-looking pair of glasses. He finally got to see her expressive chocolate brown eyes and noticed a light spatter of freckles across her nose. She occupied his mind ever since they met and finally being that close to her sent his emotions into overdrive.

They followed the narrow walkway towards the street where his car was parked. Shelby walked ahead of him and every few steps, she glanced over her shoulder and smiled. Her cherry red lips made him want to kiss her right then and there but all he did was wink flirtatiously.

She squealed with delight and clapped excitedly when they reached his car. He frowned, wondering what exactly had caused her to react that way.

"Is this yours?" she asked, pointing to his car.

"Yep."

"A sixty-nine Mustang," she whispered as she ran her

fingers reverently along the car's body, taking in every single detail. It was almost as if she was worshipping it.

"You know what car this is?" he asked.

She nodded.

Garridan opened the passenger side door and she smiled bashfully as she settled into the deep leather seat. When he got into the driver's side, he glanced at her.

"Sorry about that," she said softly as her brow furrowed.

"What's wrong?"

She shrugged. "It's just that I've loved the Mach One for as long as I can remember and the closest I ever get to one is at car shows."

"You love cars?" he asked.

"I spent a lot of time with my dad when I was little and I developed my love for cars because of him."

Garridan nodded. "Let me guess, he named you."

"Yes, he did," Shelby laughed. "She really is beautiful, Garridan. Sorry for being all giddy about her," she said apologetically before looking away.

Garridan loved his car. He salvaged her from the junkyard and rebuilding her was his passion. He'd always wanted a woman who appreciated his car, or at least understood his love for it. But he'd never met anyone like that. Until Shelby.

"You don't ever have to apologise to me for appreciating beautiful things. And thank you for saying she's beautiful. I built her myself and had the interior restored at a vintage car specialist here in Miami. One of the reasons I'm here is to collect her."

People often complimented his car, but Shelby's praise

was very flattering. A nd w hen s he l ooked b ack a t him with her pretty eyes, his heart fluttered. His body's reaction to her caught him off guard. She did things to him that he'd never felt before. Things h e d idn't q uite understand. And he absently wondered what other surprises she had in store.

SHELBY

Shelby's heart did multiple somersaults. She absolutely loved that Garridan understood her appreciation of his car. There was something very alluring about a man who knew his way around cars and before Garridan, she had never met anyone who could actually rebuild one, much less a shiny, black Mustang.

She stared into Garridan's crystal blue eyes. A look passed over them as they burrowed into her soul. She couldn't tear herself away from his gaze and wished she could lean in and kiss him. Despite the crush she'd had on him for the longest time, she'd only known him for a couple of days and he was already undoing her in ways she never thought was possible. She prayed her expression wasn't revealing her emotions too much.

Garridan dragged his eyes away from her and cleared his throat before starting the car. He looked over at her again as the car roared to life and vibrated beneath them. She danced in her seat and giggled.

He chuckled. "Ready?"

"Yes!" she exclaimed, barely able to contain her excitement.

Garridan sped off into the road, and on to making one of Shelby's wildest dreams come true.

Shelby was in awe of Miami's beauty. Because Garridan had been there many times before, he assumed the role of

Shelby's tour guide and they spent a few hours sightseeing. He drove around showing her the different landmarks and attractions on the list she and Harlow had prepared, and explained their significance as best he could. She loved how enthusiastic and informative he was, and appreciated how much effort he put into making her day special. She thought about Harlow and wished she was there, but she was glad her cousin had preparations of her own to make after being asked out on a date by a handsome local they'd met at a bar the night before.

Later on, they visited a few of the museums and memorials. They walked hand in hand, chatting comfortably as Shelby got acquainted with the city. So far, their date was more than she could have hoped for. He was a perfect gentleman, always courteous and considerate.

Although he wore a baseball cap and sunglasses, people occasionally recognised him and asked for his autograph or a picture with him. When that happened, Shelby assumed the role of photographer.

"I'm sorry about this," he whispered in her ear when a little boy handed his phone to her.

"I don't mind," she smiled. "Say cheese."

At midday, they returned to his car and made their way to the beach. On the way there, he pointed out a club.

"I'd like to bring you and Harlow here on the Fourth if you're free."

Shelby peered at the club with interest. "I don't remember when last I've been to a club. I think I'd feel out of place."

"A friend of mine is performing in a show that night.

It's for a good cause," he said, taking his eyes off the road briefly as he waited for her to reply.

"Do you dance?" she asked. She remembered movie scenes in which he showcased his athleticism and fighting skills, but she couldn't picture him dancing.

He chuckled. "Not in the way you're imagining."

"Good, because I don't either," she laughed. "I'd love to go with you. But I'll have to check with Harlow about her plans. Would you mind if she brought a date?"

"Not at all," he said and took her hand in his, lacing their fingers together.

Shelby turned her attention back to the sights before her and sighed softly as she pinched her eyes closed. She tried hard to control her runaway thoughts and the rush of emotions she felt. She needed to pull herself together because she was returning to South Africa in a few days' time. She couldn't allow her feelings for him to grow.

When Garridan finally parked, they grabbed their things from the car and made their way to the beach. And as they waded through multitudes of people who all appeared to be making the most of the gorgeous weather, he wrapped an arm around Shelby's waist and held her close.

"I prefer this part of the beach. Not many people come up here because of the rocks," he said when they headed down a short flight of stairs which led to a spot set back from where the rest of the beachgoers were. "There's less chance of me being recognised."

The view was incredible: soft, white sand; calm, turquoise waters; and palm trees in the distance. They kicked off their shoes and Garridan pitched a humongous umbrella while Shelby laid their towels side by side in its shade. Garridan was engrossed in his task, so Shelby took advantage of his distraction and quickly slipped into a pair of shorts. She wore a swimsuit under her clothes to make it easier to change, but she didn't feel brave enough to show off its high-cut bottom design and the shorts would provide a sense of modesty.

When Garridan was done, he peered up and down the beach before taking cover behind the umbrella and shed his jeans. He winked at Shelby as he tugged a green board shorts over his boxer briefs and started unbuttoning his shirt.

Shelby gaped at his casualness and how at ease he seemed to be around her. When he finally removed his shirt, her heart lurched against her chest as she took in the work of art before her. Seeing him like that in real life was more thrilling than it was watching him in movies. There were subtle differences and it eased Shelby's reservations about her own changing body. But even so, Garridan was still beautifully toned, and he had a gorgeous golden tan that stood out against the white beach and blue ocean behind him. His legs were muscular and defined. Shelby swallowed hard and tore her eyes away quickly before he caught her staring.

She followed his lead and lifted her dress over her head, tossing it beside his discarded clothes. She could feel his eyes on her, so she pretended to busy herself with something inside her bag.

GARRIDAN

Garridan watched as Shelby bent over to dig in her oversized beach bag. Her royal blue swimsuit was striking against her skin that resembled creamy latte. The top was strapless on one side, but had two thick straps reaching from one cup over her chest and across the other shoulder. He couldn't help but notice how flattering the style was on her. Her shorts covered just enough to protect her modesty but not enough to stop his mind from wandering.

She stood back up holding a tube of sunscreen and when she smeared the white cream on her skin, Garridan quickly looked away, shaking off his wayward thoughts. To distract himself, he went to the cooler box for some drinks.

"Thirsty? I don't know what you drink, so I got these," he said. "Or if you prefer, I have water too."

She pushed her sunglasses onto her forehead and looked thoughtfully at the selection. "I'll have one of these," she said, taking a raspberry soda. "Thank you."

"You're welcome."

Throughout the day, Garridan noticed how grateful Shelby was, even for the smallest of gestures. It was obvious to him how different she was to every other woman he'd dated. What they expected or demanded, she saw as a token, a gift. He reached for her hand and gently coaxed her to sit on the towels next to him. She smiled and joined him eagerly. They sat in silence for a long time, watching the waves and taking in the scenery around them.

From behind the dark lenses of his sunglasses, Garridan watched Shelby. She looked so calm and peaceful. She didn't need constant conversation to feel accepted, but she wasn't quiet or indifferent. He enjoyed her company. She didn't throw herself at him but she wasn't closed or cut-off either. Her simple touches during the day told him she was aware of his presence, and it meant more to him physically and emotionally than any exaggerated display of affection ever did. And the way she said his name undid him in ways he didn't understand.

She obviously knew he was an actor because she didn't seem surprised by the attention he'd received. And it didn't bother her when fans interrupted their day for an autograph. But did she know who exactly he was? If she did, she didn't let on and she certainly didn't want a piece of the fame. She didn't insist on being part of the photo when his fans asked for one, but offered to take them instead. Quincy also hadn't contacted him about news of them on social media where she'd surreptitiously posted a sneaky picture and tagged him. If she knew who he was, she kept it to herself and treated him like an everyday Joe. He absolutely loved that about her.

He took the sunscreen she was holding and opened the lid. "Will you?" he asked, gesturing to his back.

"Sure," she said blandly.

He smiled as her cheeks flushed a pretty shade of pink, and he was positive it had nothing to do with the warm weather. He turned away from her and tried to control his breathing as she gently spread the cream on his back. Her touch was light, tentative, and her breath was warm on his shoulder. Goosebumps flowered on his arms and his emotions were sent into a spiral.

"Thank you," he said quickly and turned to face her before she noticed the effect she had on him.

She smiled and rubbed the residual cream on the top of her thighs. "You're welcome."

"Can I ask you something personal?"

"Sure. Anything," she said and adjusted her position to give him her full attention.

"Why are you single?"

She bit her lip and doodled in the sand before telling him about meeting her children's father in high school. And after being together for nearly six years, she thought they were in a happy and committed relationship until he started acting out of character and disappearing for hours at a time.

"A few months after our last son was born, I found out he was cheating," she said. "I suddenly understood why he didn't marry me. The following day, he packed his bags and left. We didn't see him again," she continued with a shrug.

"You say *we*. Didn't the kids see him?"

She shook her head. "When he left me, he left us all. It's been so long, I don't even think about it anymore. I had dreams and goals when I met him but those were replaced by babies. And when he left, I devoted my entire being to providing for my boys so they'd never feel the absence of a father."

"It must've been tough," said Garridan.

"It was, but having three little mouths to feed is great motivation. Everything I did was for them," she said. "They're building lives of their own now, but I'd make those sacrifices all over again if I had to."

Deep down, Garridan wanted to punch the loser for doing what he did to Shelby. He couldn't imagine causing her that much pain, but could tell she wasn't hurt by it anymore.

"Your sons are blessed to have you," he said.

"Thank you, Garridan. I appreciate that."

"Do you want to speak about something else?"

"Yes, please."

They didn't speak. They sat in silence, lost in their thoughts. Normally it would've bothered Garridan, but the silence between them was comfortable, calming, even after the intensity of what she'd just shared with him.

"I really enjoy being with you," Garridan said suddenly, breaking the silence.

Shelby looked over at him. He was looking down, playing with a piece of thread on one of the towels. She wondered if he was uncomfortable expressing his feelings.

"I love being with you too," she said. "I can't remember a time I ever felt so at ease with anyone."

He looked at her. She wished she could look into his eyes instead of at her reflection in his sunglasses, so she reached out and removed them from his face. He didn't stop her, so she did the same with her own sunglasses, leaving nothing to hide their emotions with.

"Don't you like speaking about your feelings?" she asked.

He shifted uncomfortably. "I've never really had the need to, you know? Women throw themselves at me all the time, not caring about how I feel." With his head hanging again, he glanced at her through his lashes. "I know it's only been a couple of days, but the fact that you're leaving soon...I don't know what to make of it. It makes me wonder if I'll ever have this again," he said, gesturing between and around them.

Shelby nodded slowly. "I've been thinking about it too, Garridan. I've always wanted this"–she mimicked his gesture–"and I can't believe I had to travel thousands of kilometres to find you and this kind of peace, only to face leaving it behind."

He shuffled closer to her and took her hand in his. "Does it scare you?" he asked, staring into her eyes.

She swallowed. "More than you know," she replied with a soft, shaky breath.

GARRIDAN

The emotion in her voice spurred him on. Without thinking, Garridan cupped his hand around her neck and drew her gently towards him. He leaned in and placed a soft kiss on her lips. Her lips puckered against his, returning his kiss with one of her own.

They separated, unlocking their lips. It was just a peck and it lasted just a moment, but it was the most emotional kiss Garridan's ever experienced. He rested his forehead against hers and closed his eyes, relishing the moment as they breathed the same air.

Hurried rustling and the all-too-familiar sound of a camera shutter came from behind them. They looked towards the beach where two women and a man stood nearby, pointing at them. The man held a camera up and snapped another photo, and the women chatted excitedly, readying their phones to do the same. Garridan yanked Shelby into his arms and pinned her against the towels, covering her body with his and burying his face in her neck. They lay there, chest to chest, until the voices behind them disappeared. When Garridan lifted his head and peered down at her, she looked up at him with an amused expression.

"What are you doing?" she asked.

He cocked an eyebrow and simply said, "Paparazzi."

Shelby laughed out loud wondering what his little stunt looked like to his admirers. Garridan joined in. His hearty laugh vibrated through her. She adored seeing him so carefree and happy.

"What do you think the headline will be?" he asked as his laughter subsided. He was lying on his stomach, hovering over her and bearing his weight on his elbows.

She pursed her lips in thought. "Um, maybe 'Garridan Luca tackles woman on Miami beach'?"

That earned her another throaty laugh. When he recovered, he looked down at her and said, "I've been wondering about something but if I ask, promise you won't think I'm being vain."

"You can always ask me anything," she said, placing her arm behind her head.

"Did you know who I was when I gave you this hat or did you only find out about me later?" His gaze searched her face before finally resting on her eyes.

She smiled. She wondered when he'd ask. "I knew the moment I saw you after you tapped my shoulder and gave me a mini heart attack."

He chuckled. "Why didn't you say anything?"

"I didn't think it was important that I knew who you were to the world. It was important for me to learn about you as a person. So, I tried to forget you're famous." This time, her eyes searched his face. "Why do you ask?"

He shrugged. "I just wondered. Most people *want* me to know they recognise me; want to impress me with their general knowledge about my life. They read things online and think they know me or have a right to me. Like the people who took the photos now." He pointed with his thumb over his shoulder. "Not many people try to get to know the actual me."

Shelby nodded. "I understand completely. I'm not famous or anything, but I feel that way when people back home make assumptions about me based on what they see or hear. I don't care about their opinions, but I resent that they feel entitled to pieces of me in some way."

"So you're a hometown celebrity?" he asked teasingly and pinched her chin affectionately between his knuckles.

"Not in the least," she replied, laughing.

"And what about this morning when we were stopped for pictures? You didn't seem annoyed by it."

She thought about it before replying. "Acting is your career, Garridan. It's what you do for a living. And the fact that you have 'fans'"–she indicated between quotes–"simply means that you're doing a very good job. I'd never do anything to ruin your reputation. You have an unwritten obligation to be friendly and accommodating when you can allow it. And photo ops are part of the deal. It's part of your job description."

"No one's ever described my acting as just another job," he smiled. "But, why do you say *'fans'* like that?" He emphasised the word and mimicked her air quotes.

She snickered. "I don't like that word. I feel it's a bit presumptuous for a celebrity to think I'm a fanatic when

I could simply appreciate his or her role in a movie, or an excellent performance. The word *fan* makes it sound like an obsession."

"So where does that leave us?"

"Can I be honest?"

"That's all I ever want."

"I appreciate that you're diverse and don't always play the same type of character. I really lose myself watching you. I love losing myself in you." Feeling self-conscious, she quickly pulled her phone from her back pocket and scrolled. "Here," she said, handing her phone to Garridan to distract him from her last comment.

He stared at it wordlessly.

"It's a list of quotes from the movies and shows you've acted in," she said and took the phone. After scrolling some more, she handed it to him again. "These are my favourites."

Shelby studied him as he stared at her phone. His expression was unreadable. He locked the phone and handed it back to her. She watched him closely as she laid it on the towel beside her. He just looked at her, gently rubbing his thumb back and forth against her jawline. They stayed that way for the longest time and she slowly grew anxious about her inadvertent confession. His silence was unnerving.

"I guess that makes me your fan," she said, her voice barely a whisper.

GARRIDAN

As Shelby stared up at him, anxiety or regret flickered across her face momentarily. Garridan realised he hadn't said anything for a long time. It was hard to, though, because of the knot in his throat, his raised heartbeat and all the other ways in which his body reacted to her gaze.

His feelings were new and sudden and, paired with the way she said she loved losing herself in him, simply overwhelming. If he said anything, his emotions would escape and there would be no holding back. She was leaving the country soon, he really needed to hold back.

He cupped her neck again and tenderly caressed her cheek and lips with his thumb. Instead of saying anything, he leaned down, closing the gap between them. He stared into the chocolate depths of her eyes and shut his own when his lips found hers. This time, he kissed her with purpose. He transferred his words, his thoughts, his feelings into that kiss and hoped she would hear and feel what he so desperately wanted her to know.

She returned his kiss. Her arms curled around his neck and pulled him closer. He obliged by embracing her and pulling her into him. He deepened their kiss and she moaned with pleasure.

When Garridan finally pulled away, Shelby's lips were swollen and red. He'd never seen anything more perfect in his life.

"Thank you," he said finally.

Her brows furrowed. "What for?"

"For being you."

It was all he was prepared to say. He drew her in for another embrace before letting her go. He loved that she didn't push him for an explanation.

She smiled up at him and asked, "Are you just gonna kiss me all day or are we going to eat?"

He laughed and tugged her up from the towels. "Let's get you fed."

Shelby was still swooning when they unpacked their lunch. She dug deep to disguise her emotions; to play it off with a laugh. The look in Garridan's eyes almost made her believe he felt something for her, but she knew it was impossible. And it was hard to pretend she wasn't affected by his kiss. It was so unexpected yet so sensual and emotional, it left her breathless. Her fingers touched her mouth. She could still feel his lips on hers.

"You okay?" he asked.

"I'm fine," she said, reminding herself not to get lost in her thoughts. And to distract herself, she focused on the incredible lunch Garridan had packed – mini chicken wraps, a medley of fruit, sweets, and mixed nuts and raisins. "This looks really good," she added.

"Well, dig in," he laughed.

Garridan did as he'd promised: a date where they could talk. They spoke about their families, growing up, hopes and dreams. For the first time in her life, Shelby felt a real connection with someone outside of her family, not fearing judgement or rejection.

"Ghostwriter?" he asked with a frown when she told him about her career. "Doesn't it bug you that you don't get recognition for your work?"

"Initially, it did," she said, thinking back to the first successful publications that will never be credited to her.

"But as time passed, I got used to it and now I actually appreciate the anonymity of it all. It helps since I don't particularly like criticism or failure when it comes to my work."

Garridan nodded. "But the beauty of failure is knowing you tried, and criticism helps you to understand where you can improve."

"That's true when it's constructive and comes from a place of kindness. But the public can be unnecessarily judgemental and callous. I'm sure you know what I mean."

"Yep, I know exactly what you mean," he said without elaborating.

He told her about starting out in Romania and how coming to the U.S. as a little boy had changed his life.

"I've often wondered where and what I would've been if my mother chose to stay in Romania," he said. "Everything amazing about my life started the day we arrived here. I was only four years old, but I remember a lot about that time."

Shelby marvelled at how a single decision on his mother's part had altered Garridan's entire existence and gave him opportunities he otherwise wouldn't have had. "And what about your father?" she asked.

"He died before I was born, so the only father I know is my stepdad. He's a really good man and he adores my mother. They're still very much in love. We've had a great life because of him."

"I'm sorry about your father. But, I'm glad your mother found someone wonderful. I love hearing stories like hers."

"Why?"

"It gives me hope that women like me can find love again."

"Anyone can find what my parents did. It just takes meeting the right person," he said, taking her hand in his.

Shelby smiled at the thought but knew it wasn't that easy.

As if he could sense her reservations, Garridan said, "Tell me more about yourself."

Her story wasn't as exciting as his but he listened intently and asked questions about life in South Africa. He sounded intrigued and promised to visit her when he was done filming his next movie.

"Why did you choose Miami?" he asked when she spoke about their vacation.

She told him about her travel dreams, and about her and Harlow's time exploring the Caribbean Islands before coming to Miami.

"The last week of our trip coincided with Independence Day, so we decided to come here to experience it. Miami just happened to be one of Harlow's dream destinations. She's a true romantic," Shelby said with a smile. "She's convinced she'll meet her soulmate on this vacation."

"What about *you*?" he asked. "Did you also have hopes of meeting your dream guy here?"

She hesitated before replying. Although she fantasised about meeting Garridan one day, coming to Miami wasn't about him; she didn't even know he'd be there.

"Not really," she finally said. "Harlow's thoughts interested me but my intentions were about doing something new. For me, the Islands were an adventure. I just love the histories, the cultures, and architecture. I wanted to experience something different."

"How do you feel about Los Angeles?"

"Well, when I was younger, I always thought I'd move to L.A. At the time, I wanted to live in a place like that especially because of how it was portrayed on TV and in movies."

"And now?"

"Now I know more about life than to believe everything I see on TV," she laughed. "I think I'd love to explore Los Angeles first before making that decision."

"You'll love L.A. and I think you'd fit right in. Do you want a test run?" he asked with a grin.

She frowned. "What do you mean?"

"It's playtime!" he said excitedly and dragged her up from the towels before running down the beach towards the sea.

She ran behind him and when she caught up, he picked her up and carried her into the water. They played in the sea for a while and raced along the beach. Later on, Garridan helped her choose seashells and rocks for her collection.

Back under the shade of the umbrella, they checked their phones for messages and Garridan surprised her when he insisted on taking a few photos together.

"Are you sure?" she asked, assuming he'd still be bitter about their recent paparazzi incident.

"Of course I'm sure. I'm asking you because I'm *your* biggest fan," he winked. "Photo ops are part of your job description."

She laughed when he used her words.

Eventually she gave in and they used his phone to capture a few photos. When they settled back onto the towels, she sat between his legs and leaned against his chest while they looked through the photos.

"Will you send me some of those please?" she asked.

He forwarded his favourites to her immediately. She heard her phone ding and thanked him without checking.

"Do you often have days like this?" she asked.

"Hardly. I don't usually have this much time to myself."

"What do you do?"

"Apart from my actual work – studying scripts, rehearsals, filming, and promoting shows and movies – I do interviews, photoshoots, and charitable work. Basically anything Marc and Quincy line up for me."

"What kind of charitable work?"

"I'm passionate about children learning to read. I'm an avid reader and it pains me to know that books are being replaced by cellphones and words, by emojis. The charities I support involve instilling a passion for reading, more especially reading *books*." He emphasised the word.

Shelby sat up and placed a gentle kiss on his cheek. "Thank you," she said simply.

Reading was an important part of her life and her love for books led to her career as a writer. It moved her that Garridan was as passionate about it as her.

"What for?" he asked.

"For being you."

He smiled when she repeated his words and kissed the crown of her hair.

As they drove towards his next surprise with the sun setting behind them, Garridan looked over at Shelby who'd been really quiet. She leaned her head against the headrest and closed her eyes.

"Tired?" he asked.

"Mmmmm."

Her reply made him smile. "We don't have to do this next thing if you're too tired. It's quite a long drive, but I can turn around and take you back to your place."

"I'm good," she mumbled. "I'm just resting my eyes."

Garridan turned on the radio. An evocative love song filled the silence and he fiddled with the dial to find something else.

"No, go back please. I love that song," Shelby said.

When he dialled back to the previous station and turned the volume up, she sang along lazily. Garridan enjoyed how at ease she seemed to be with him. They drove the rest of the way with only the radio playing in the background. He used the quiet time to reflect on their day and revelled in his contentment. He couldn't recall a time when he felt more at home with anyone and he wondered if his other relationships didn't work because he was waiting for the kind of connection he had with Shelby.

But like a damper on his spirits, he remembered her impending departure. He looked over at his sleeping beauty and his heart pinched at the sight of her. So obliviously pretty. Sweet as anything and so much more than he could have asked for. He was definitely going to miss the hell out of her when she left.

About half a mile from their destination, he patted her shoulder gently to rouse her. "We're nearly there."

Shelby sat up and rubbed her eyes as she craned her neck to peer through the windows around her. "It's so dark," she said.

They were travelling on a dirt road. Garridan drove slowly, careful not to kick stones up from under the tyres onto the car's bodywork. And after a few minutes, he watched as Shelby's face lit up. When she looked at him again, an expression he didn't recognise crossed her face. Her gaze tugged at his heart and something inside him snapped. Garridan wished he could take a photo of her like that, so he could have a reminder of the moment he wanted to give his heart away for the first time.

They were in the middle of nowhere with only a log cabin coming into view ahead of them.

"How did you know?" Shelby asked.

Garridan wouldn't have missed the tremble of her voice, but she didn't care. In the short time she'd known him, he'd managed to make her feel so special that her emotions were in turmoil.

"I asked Harlow," he confessed. "She told me you've always wanted to spend a weekend in a cabin, away from civilisation, but you've never had the chance to." He parked in front of the house. "I can't promise you a weekend, but we're staying overnight. I hope it's okay?"

She started to nod but suddenly remembered, "I don't have any other clothes to change into!"

He placed a hand on her knee. "Don't worry. It's all taken care of. Everything you need is already here." He opened the door and walked over to her side. "Come on, let's go inside."

She held his hand and they ascended the three steps onto the veranda which led to a red wooden door. It looked new and out of place against the house's weather-worn wood around it.

Garridan took a key out from under a rock and unlocked the door. He opened his arms dramatically and said, "Welcome to your home for the night!" and with a flourish, he scooped Shelby into his arms.

She squealed as he playfully joggled her. The smile on his face outshone the full moon in the distance behind him. He was so beautiful, he took her breath away every time she looked at him. And the more time she spent with him, the more she feared going home.

"Garridan," she said, stroking the hair along his jaw. "I wished for you for so long," she added, not caring to hide her feelings.

His face softened as he gazed at her and he placed feather soft kisses on her lips before he carried her over the threshold like a newlywed couple. Once inside, he used his foot to shut the door behind them.

He dropped her legs, carefully cradling her body against his as her feet found the floor. His heart drummed rapidly beneath her fingertips. His eyes were alive with emotion and she wished she knew what it meant. He ran his hands slowly down the side of her face, her neck, her shoulders, her arms, then around her waist, locking his fingers in the arch of her back.

They stood staring at each other, neither uttering a word. Her eyes found his lips, yearning for his kiss. The anticipation was driving her insane but she wanted to wait, to draw the moment out because she desperately needed to hold on to every precious second of their time together.

Garridan closed his eyes and lowered his forehead against hers. He took deep breaths. Beneath her fingers, his racing heart slowed down.

"What are you thinking?" he asked. "Be honest."

"I'm thinking about how I'm falling for you. How much I'm dreading going home."

His embrace tightened around her and he whispered, "Tell me more."

"I've never met anyone like you," she declared. "And if I never see you again, I'll spend the rest of my life searching for you in other people."

He caressed her hair as she clung to him. He murmured sweet words of surrender, telling her how beautiful she was and how his heart was feeling something real for the first time.

"What am I gonna do when you're gone?" he asked in a strained voice.

They stood quietly in each other's arms for what seemed like hours when Garridan eventually broke the silence. "You must be hungry," he said, taking her hand in his and walking to the kitchen.

"I am, actually," she realised. "What do you have here?"

He opened the fridge and retrieved a large glass dish covered in foil. They peeked inside and saw what looked like a delicious lasagne. Shelby's stomach growled and they both laughed.

"Who helped you with our lunch and tonight's meal?" she asked curiously while she placed some of the food into the microwave. She didn't think about asking him earlier.

He shrugged sheepishly. "I packed our lunch but Marc's fiancée, Megan, made the wraps and the lasagne. She's kinda my unofficial assistant."

"Did they help you arrange everything we did today?"

"Yeah. I called in some favours," he confessed.

Shelby laughed as she settled onto the counter. "And Harlow? Does she know I'm sleeping over?"

"She does. She packed your overnight bag. Megan collected it from her sometime today and brought it here."

Shelby could only stare at him. It astounded her that someone who barely knew her could be so thoughtful and considerate of her needs. "You really thought about everything, didn't you?"

He crossed the kitchen to where she sat and planted himself between her legs, his hands rested lightly on her hips. "Did I overstep?" he asked. "Is it too much?"

Shaking her head, she slid her arms around his neck and looked into his eyes. "Everything is perfect. I love every second of today. No one's ever done anything like this for me. Thank you. And I'm grateful to everyone who helped."

Relief washed over Garridan. Knowing Shelby enjoyed the day and she didn't begrudge his efforts made him feel proud. "You're very welcome," he said with a smile.

The aroma wafting through the kitchen beckoned them and they shuffled around getting plates and forks ready. Shelby dished generous portions for both of them. She also added some of the salad she found in the fridge. Garridan looked at the massive serving and wondered whether she'd be able to finish it all, especially considering that she ate so much at the beach.

They carried their plates to the living room where they sat on the floor in front of the unlit fireplace. They enjoyed their delicious meal in silence. Garridan watched Shelby while she ate. He could picture a life like that with her. She made him miss something he didn't know was gone.

As if she could feel his eyes on her, she turned to look at him. She tilted her head slightly and a mischievous smile crossed her face.

He cocked an eyebrow and asked, "What are you thinking?"

He sensed her embarrassment as she dipped her head, but she answered anyway. "Did Megan leave bubble bath?"

Garridan immediately jumped up. Abandoning his food, he stalked down the passage and returned quickly with a bottle of bubble bath. He waggled his eyebrows and Shelby broke into a fit of laughter.

"I'll be right back," he said

A few seconds later, she heard water running. While she waited, she thought about her time with Garridan and touched her lips again. She used to lose herself in him while watching him act and remembered that when he kissed a co-star, she'd wish it was her. Beyond the movies, she came across videos on the internet of him interacting with others – his sweet and considerate ways, how he engaged his supporters, the high praise other actors gave him as a person. She prayed for someone like him and now she was there; not with someone *like* him, but actually him. She was going to spend the night with the man of her dreams.

She had no idea where her sudden brazenness had come from when she agreed to spend the night, but her courage slowly waned as she continued picking at the food on her plate, too nervous to think about what lay ahead.

Garridan didn't return after he started filling the tub and Shelby wondered what he was up to. "Garridan?" she called.

"Don't come in here just yet!" he shouted from deep inside the cabin.

"Okay," she said.

He returned a few minutes later, held out his hand and wordlessly led her to the bathroom.

The small room was steamy and smelled like berries. Luxurious bubbles filled the tub and dim candlelight provided a relaxing atmosphere.

"This is really great, Garridan," she said, smiling up at him. She really needed to unwind after the day they'd had.

He stood in front of her, caressing her arms. A troubled look crossed his features and Shelby's heart sank to the pit of her stomach. She worried he was going to break things off with her, but instantly felt silly about the direction of her thoughts. There was nothing between them. Nothing to break off. There could be nothing more than just that one unbelievable day. The fairy tale would've had to end at some point.

Shelby clenched her hands together and braced herself for the inevitable. "What's wrong?" she asked.

He smiled reassuringly and replied, "Nothing's wrong. But I do want to ask you something."

"You know you can ask me anything."

He let out an exasperated breath before taking a deep one. "Can we bathe together?" The words tumbled out of his mouth as if he wanted to get it over with.

Shelby gasped. "Gar–"

"You can leave your swimsuit on," he interjected. "I don't know when we'll have another chance to be together this way, babe. I want to experience as much as possible with you before you leave." He sucked in a breath. "I feel like I'm running out of time."

She smiled at the term of endearment and considered his request. He was right. They only had that moment. Maybe there'd be other dates before they left Miami, but that moment in that house at that time was all they had.

She nodded. "Okay."

Garridan drew her into his arms and whispered a quick thank you. "We should get in before the water goes cold. Turn around so I can get undressed." He studied her face. "Unless you want to watch," he teased.

Calling his bluff, she folded her arms across her chest challengingly. She cocked an eyebrow and waited.

Garridan shrugged.

Her jaw dropped. Although she'd already seen him do it earlier at the beach, this performance was nothing like the previous one. Garridan's faced morphed into a smouldering masterpiece. His eyes burned into hers and his lips parted as he unbuttoned his shirt slowly. Deliberately. His body pulsed to an inaudible beat. She wasn't sure if she was imagining it, but, it looked as though he was moving in slow motion.

He opened the front of his shirt and ran a hand slowly down his body from his hair, across his chest, down to his belt, oozing sex appeal. He peeled his shirt from his body, first one sleeve then the next and tossed it to Shelby who let it fall to the floor. She was in no state to function like a normal, lucid human being.

She swallowed hard when he unbuckled his belt and kicked off his shoes. He undid the buttons of his jeans. One. By. One. He sucked a breath between his teeth and bit his bottom lip. And when he finally dragged the denim over his hips, she couldn't stop the moan that escaped her.

Garridan's sudden burst of laughter yanked Shelby out of her stupor.

"It's not funny!" she complained, feeling a blush rise in her cheeks. She swatted his arm playfully.

He grabbed her hand, pulling her against him. "Basic roleplay, sweetheart. I'm an actor, remember?" he said, giving her a quick peck on the cheek before stripping down completely and jumping into the tub.

After his impromptu striptease, Garridan was sprawled in the bathtub waiting for Shelby. He swiped at the bubbles around the rim of the tub and blew them into the air.

When she finally returned to the bathroom, she looked slightly more composed than she did during his performance. She wore a fleecy bathrobe and fluffy slippers, and her hair was tied back into a ponytail. She was so damn adorable.

She stood in front of the tub and looked at him. He smiled longingly at her, silently willing her to jump into the water with him. On cue, she loosened the belt of her bathrobe. The front parted and she let it slide slowly down her naked body. His eyes raked over her bare, sun-kissed skin. Garridan was not expecting that at all. He assumed she would've worn her swimsuit. He swallowed hard as she stepped into the tub and lowered herself between his legs. She sat facing him, the bubbles barely covering the breasts he tried desperately not to look at.

"Hi," she said finally. Her face was flushed and her breath was shallow.

"Hi," he said in a deep, raspy voice that didn't sound like his.

Thankfully, she turned around and nestled into him. He breathed a little easier now that he wasn't being hypnotised.

"You didn't wear your suit," he said, to break the awkward silence.

She smirked. "You know what they say: if you can't beat 'em, join 'em."

They laughed and finally relaxed and enjoyed the soothing bath. Shelby played soft music from her phone and they chatted more about their lives, their interests, their passion, and what they wished for the future.

When a country singer crooned a sorrowful song, Shelby sang along. The words were haunting and so relevant to their situation. She turned to face him as she sang the chorus about cherishing their time together and holding onto the memories. As the melody faded out, she nestled into him again and placed a gentle kiss in the palm of his hand. The simple act spoke so much about her feelings for him that Garridan's pounding heart nearly burst through his chest.

He didn't know where all these overwhelming feelings came from and he didn't understand why she had such a strong hold on his emotions. But what he did know was that she'd be leaving the country soon and probably wouldn't come back. It was a fluke that he'd met her and before him, nothing bound her to this country. What if he never saw her again? What if she left and someone else got to share moments like these with her? The emotion in her eyes when he held her in his arms earlier nearly pushed him over the edge. They'd just met and only spent one day together, was it crazy that he felt like they'd been in love with each other for years? Was he prepared to live with the consequences of letting her go?

"Stay with me," he said.

"I am," she nodded as she drew bubbly circles in his palm.

He closed his hand around hers. "No, I mean stay here with me. Don't go back home to South Africa."

Shelby tensed against him. "Garridan, you know I can't. I have a life, kids, obligations back home. I can't just stay." After a beat, she added, "But God knows how much I want to."

He moved to sit in front of her, splashing water onto the floor. "Shelby, you can fulfil all those obligations from here. You told me your sons are grown and busy living their own lives. Besides, once you're settled here, they can come and live with us or we can set them up in their own apartments. Please, baby, just please stay?"

He hadn't prayed in a long time, but he quickly prayed she'd say yes.

Shelby couldn't wrap her mind around what was happening. She wasn't prepared for that at all. She was usually a step ahead, always had a plan and a backup plan. But now she drew a blank. Her mind was a muddled mess.

On the one hand, this was everything she'd ever wanted – to be with Garridan and start a brand-new life there. But it was just a fantasy; she never thought it could ever happen. On the other hand, she couldn't just uproot her entire life and relinquish her responsibilities for something she wasn't even sure would work. If it didn't, what would happen then?

"Shelby?" Garridan said, breaking into her thoughts.

She sighed. "Garridan, I don't fit into your world." She spoke cautiously. "I'm not *from* your world. I'm not glamorous or famous, or even the least bit interested in all that attention. I'm a very private person and this"–she pointed around the room–"what we had today, and having a job and being normal, is more my speed."

"I know. I *know* all that. And that's exactly what I want too," he said earnestly, cupping her face in his hands. "Look, I'll always be an actor and the things that come with it will always follow me, you said it yourself. But off-screen, this is all I want. At the end of the day, I want to come home to an amazingly adorable woman and my amazingly chilled life and unwind. I have obligations too and we won't have to go to every event but when everything is over, I want to come home to this. To us." He took her hands in his and held it to his chest in silent plea.

He sounded so convincing, she almost said yes. "You've never had this before. It's new and different, but what if the novelty wears off and you get bored? What if you get criticised about your unglamorous partner? What if I embarrass you?"

He chuckled. "You'll never embarrass me. Look at me," he said, stroking the smattering of silver strands in his dark beard. "I'm forty-four years old and I've accomplished all I'd set out to professionally. But I'm ready for the next phase of my life. I don't need glamorous, I need home and you feel like home to me." He smiled at her. "And you obviously have no clue how beautiful you are, so I guarantee you now that the tabloids will only speak about the new mysterious beauty on my arm. Please?" he asked, kissing the tip of her nose.

She sighed again. A headache was forming behind her eyes. She needed more time before she could decide. "Can I at least think about it?"

Garridan nodded and brought her to his chest in an affectionate embrace. "Thank you," he said.

Without another word, he stepped out of the tub and wrapped a towel around his waist. He grabbed another towel for Shelby who was still grappling with her thoughts.

"Ready?" he asked as he opened the towel for her.

She nodded and stepped out of the tub and into his arms.

He held her hand as they walked to the bedroom.

Shelby sat on the bed and watched as Garridan discarded his wet towel and put on a fresh set of clothes. Once again, she thought about how obviously comfortable he was around her. It was as if they'd done it a thousand times before, and as if dressing and undressing in front of each other was the most natural thing in the world to them.

"What are you thinking?" he asked when he caught her staring. He was rubbing the towel through his wet hair.

"I wear the same thing to bed back home," she said, pointing to his sweatpants.

He smiled brightly. "Really? And what do you have now?"

She shrugged. "I don't know. Harlow packed my bag, remember? The bathrobe and slippers aren't mine, they look new. Let's see what she packed for me to sleep in."

Shelby searched the small suitcase that was left in the room for her. She laughed when she found a racy black lace nightgown that looked more like a top. She held it up for Garridan to see and a massive smile spread across his face.

She tossed it at him and said, "Not gonna happen."

He laughed but continued to gawk at the scrap of material in his hand. She finally found something a bit more her taste – leggings and a long-sleeved t-shirt. She guessed it wasn't meant for sleeping in but she wasn't going to spend her first and probably only night with Garridan with her butt sticking out while she sleeps. What was Harlow thinking?

Shelby threw the towel in the hamper Garridan had used earlier, and got dressed. She noticed him watching her but unlike before, she wasn't self-conscious. If that was the only night she got with him, she wasn't going to waste it on silly little inhibitions. She was going to live in the moment and leave with no regrets or what ifs.

GARRIDAN

Watching Shelby as she got ready for bed stirred something in Garridan. His heart raced. It was a simple act and her clothes were plain, but in that moment, she couldn't have been more beautiful. He looked down at the lacy thing in his hand and put it on the nightstand beside him. She didn't need scanty sleepwear to be sexy.

He plumped his pillow and leaned back into it while he watched her get on with her night-time routine. He smiled. He wanted this. With her. As much as his request in the bathroom had stunned Shelby, it surprised him too. After spending time with her, he craved more and dreaded her leaving, but he didn't plan on asking her to stay; it just happened. But as spontaneous as it all was, he didn't regret asking and he was relieved she was going to think about it. Again, he prayed she'd say yes. He understood her concerns but he'd seen the other side, the glam, the fame, it will always be there. This was rare. This didn't come around twice.

Shelby was sitting at the mirror dabbing balm on her lips. She looked so at ease. She was more comfortable with him than she was earlier and his heart swelled at the realisation. He recalled his ex-relationships and wondered how he'd put up with all the drama that came with it – the constant need for attention, the social media obsession, the list went on. Being with Shelby really was a different experience.

He suddenly wondered if that was what she feared; the unpredictability of his life. Is that what he would be dragging her into? Would the roles be reversed in a way that he would be the one bringing drama into her peaceful life? Will she sit on a bed one day and compare him to her exes and wonder how she put up with him? Doubt that wasn't present when he asked her to stay started creeping in. What if she said yes and ended up hating it here? What if she got tired of his obligations and his absence when he was away filming? What if...

"Don't," Shelby said from beside him.

He was so caught up in his thoughts, he didn't even notice her coming to bed. "Don't what?" he asked.

"Don't overthink it. Let's just enjoy the rest of tonight and sleep on it. We'll speak about it when we're both ready."

He smiled and snuggled in next to her. "Okay," he said, kissing her cheek. "What do you wanna do?"

She grabbed her phone from the nightstand. "I need to check in with my family before they start their day. Do you mind?"

"Not at all. Can I watch?"

She giggled, "Of course."

She texted Harlow to let her know she was okay and Harlow replied that she was still out with her date, Rodrigo. She then made some video calls to her family back home. Her sons spoke about what they did the day before and she told them a little about Miami. Her mother assured her she was fine and that Shelby should enjoy the rest of her vacation. When she ended the call, she kissed her phone's screen.

Garridan pulled her into him and held her close. The love she felt for her family radiated off her in waves and he wanted to bask in it. He wanted her to love him that way too. She squeezed him as if she could read his thoughts.

"You have a beautiful family," he said after a while.

He felt her smile against his chest. "Thank you."

She hesitated and he could sense there was more she wanted to say.

"What is it?" he asked eventually.

"Isn't that something you want too?"

"What?" he asked.

"Kids. A family of your own." She lifted her head to look at him. "I can't give you that, you know? I don't want any more children."

He nodded. "I've thought about it. Our worlds really are different. You chose to have kids when you were young, so you can enjoy your life now that they're older and you're still young enough to have fun. While as actors, we have to make the most of our youth and build on that while we can. We tend to have children when we're older."

"I know lots of people who think the way you do," Shelby said. "I see the merit in both scenarios. But that doesn't answer my question."

"Honestly, I don't know how to answer that question. I've never thought I'd be in this situation. Most women I know are prepared to have kids at the age of fifty. It's not unusual. But I guess it's only because they don't already have children." He sighed. This conversation was giving him a headache. "Can we talk about something else?"

"Please," she replied.

They chatted about interesting things they'd read and about their favourite books. Garridan asked Shelby for her social media handles. She already followed his public accounts, so he added her on his private ones which were under a pseudonym. He explained it was a way for him to share the more personal and intimate parts of his life with his family and close friends.

"Do you post your own stuff on your public accounts?" she asked.

"Sometimes. Mostly when it's personal, like pictures I take while on vacation or sending wishes on significant holidays. It's a nice way to connect with my fans."

"I've seen actors delete posts about aspects of movies they weren't allowed to share. Did that ever happen to you?"

"Never. I'm very careful about what I post. Occasionally, we're allowed to share tidbits of what's happening on set. It's part of promotion and keeps the fans' expectations high. But Quincy's wife manages my professional online presence and makes sure the posts fulfil contractual conditions. She also monitors the public's reception to my roles or performances, and fills me in on anything I'd like to address personally."

"It all sounds really exciting," Shelby said.
"I guess it is. They haven't threatened to resign yet," Garridan laughed.

They checked the social media accounts they followed

and discussed posts they saw, and Shelby shared some of her favourite quotes with him. Everything they did felt so natural. Garridan enjoyed how effortless their connection was.

As time passed, they grew more and more tired. It had been a long day.

"Tired?" he asked when she stifled yet another yawn.

She nodded.

"Okay, let's sleep," he said in a low voice.

He tucked her under his arm and they shared a passionate goodnight kiss. Before Garridan knew it, she was fast asleep.

He stared down at his sleeping beauty. "Please stay," he said one more time before he turned off the bedside lamp and fell asleep.

An urgent need to use the bathroom woke Garridan. He blinked and looked around the room. At first, he wasn't sure where he was, but the fruity scent and soft warmth in his arms reminded him.

It was still dark. Shelby was pinned against him with an arm draped across his waist. She looked so peaceful, he didn't want to disturb her sleep. He adjusted his body and slowly slid his arm out from under her. As soon as he was free, he slipped into the bathroom.

When he returned, he crept back into bed beside her. He laid his head on the pillow and faced her where she slept in a pool of moonlight. Her long hair was splayed out around her and a few silky curls covered her face. Garridan gently brushed the hair from her face causing her to stir, but she didn't wake up. She mumbled something un-intelligible. He realised she was dreaming and drew closer to hear what she was saying. She muttered again, but this time slightly clearer, and he gasped. He wished he knew what she was dreaming because she said, "Garridan, wait for me."

When Shelby woke up, the sun was shining brightly through the window. Garridan was sleeping peacefully next to her, so she kissed his cheek lightly and went to the bathroom, careful not to wake him.

She brushed her teeth and pinned her hair into a bun on top of her head before going to the kitchen in search of coffee and something to eat. While she waited for the coffee to brew and the previous night's leftovers to warm up in the microwave, she smiled as she recalled how wonderful it was to wake up next to Garridan.

She filled mugs with coffee, dished lasagne into a plate for them to share, and padded to the bedroom to wake him. She wasn't sure what his plans were for the day, so she wanted him to eat before he left. Placing the tray on the nightstand, she crawled across the bed and sat next to him.

"Garridan," she nudged him gently and waited a bit. "Garridan," she said again, nudging him more forcefully.

He groaned and reached out for her, pulling her into his arms and nuzzling her. She giggled as his beard tickled her neck.

"I brought breakfast," she said in hopes it would lure him out of bed.

"Coffee?" he asked.

"Yep."

It was all he needed to hear. He sat up against the headboard and held out his hand to take the mug from her. "Good morning," he said after one sip.

"Good morning. Not a morning person?" she asked, watching him as she ate a forkful of food. He was so adorable. His hair was dishevelled and his eyes were still sleepy.

"I usually am, but it's not every day I get to sleep next to a beautiful woman," he said dryly. "I actually thought I was dreaming and didn't want to wake up."

Shelby smiled, but her heart skipped several beats and she felt a flutter in her stomach. Only he had this effect on her. "Did you sleep well then?"

He swallowed his mouthful of food. "Better than I have in a really long time. How about you?"

She nodded. "Me too. Thank you again so much for yesterday. Everything was perfect."

"I think I'm the one who must thank you. It was a first for me. Did you have any dreams?"

She frowned as she thought about it. "I don't know," she replied, sipping on her coffee. "If I did, I can't remember. Do you have meetings today?"

"I do," he sighed. "I have an interview – a talk show appearance – at the studio at one thirty. What's the time?"

Shelby checked her phone. "Seven fifteen."

"Are you in a rush to leave?" he asked.

She shook her head. "Harlow and I have plans for this afternoon, so I'm in no hurry."

"What are you gonna do?"

"We were supposed to go on a boat tour this morning

and gift shopping later. But Rodrigo will take my place on the boat. I'll join her for shopping."

"Did you give him your spot because of me? Because you had to sleep over?"

"No. I wanted her to have what we had yesterday. Don't feel bad about our sleepover."

"That's really sweet of you," he said, smiling.

"She's amazing. I want her to be happy."

"Come here," he said as he placed his empty cup on the nightstand.

She crawled to him and he took her in his arms.

"Can I kiss you?" he whispered.

She squirmed as desire flashed in his eyes. "I think we're past the asking stage," she whispered back. And she closed her eyes as he claimed her mouth.

Garridan took full advantage of Shelby's acceptance of him. He simply loved her easy-going nature and the fact that she was so easy to love. He adored her. Everything about her made him feel like they were made for each other.

He knew they were both waiting to resume their discussions about her staying and him wanting children. He knew that since he was the one who asked her to stay, he should be the one to raise it first. But he was scared. Since he'd considered his request from her perspective, he was afraid she'd say no and he'd lose her forever. But he also worried that she'd say yes and resent him later. He didn't know how to deal with it.

But for now, he was kissing her. He relished the feel of her in his arms and the way she felt pressed up against him. He loved her pleasurable little moans and the way she ran her fingers through the hair at the nape of his neck. When his body awakened, he slowed their kiss and eventually broke it. He didn't want to, but he had to stop. Shelby was nothing like some of the women he'd been with. Sleeping next to her was indescribable, unlike anything he'd experienced before. Despite his desire, he didn't want to rush things with her.

When they broke apart, she sighed.

"What's wrong?" he asked as he got up from the bed and

distracted himself by gathering his clothes from the day before.

"Nothing. I just think I'm going to miss you today," she said as she slipped out of the bed.

He chuckled. "I *know* I'm going to miss you," he said and swatted her butt playfully.

She squealed and fell back onto the bed.

His heart clenched at the way she was looking at him. "Can I call you later?" he asked.

She smirked. "I think we're past the asking stage," she repeated her earlier thought.

He winked and turned towards the bathroom.

A few hours later, Garridan left his hotel room and headed out to the studio. He was ahead of schedule, so he visited the hotel's jewellery store to place a special order. As he left the store, his phone dinged with a message. It was from Quincy: *I'm at the studio. Have you seen this?* A second later, an image filled the screen. It was a tabloid article. The title read *IS THIS LOVE?* followed by a photo of him and Shelby at the beach. Their heads were melded together and he was cupping her neck intimately. The photo was captioned: *Garridan Luca and unknown female in intimate moment*

Garridan replied: *No, I haven't. Thanks for the heads up*

He wondered if Shelby had seen it already and decided to send it to her before she found out from someone else.

Guilt instantly overcame Shelby when she saw the picture Garridan had sent her. She replied to his text:
I'm sorry, Garridan

What are you sorry for? His reply came quickly.

I took off your sunglasses. That's why they recognised you. I shouldn't have done that

It's not your fault. his happens all the time. I just don't want you to be caught off guard in case anyone recognises you from that picture. Okay?

Okay. I doubt they will but thank you

I have to go now but I'll call you after the show. And don't forget to ask Harlow about tomorrow

She looked at the picture again and shook her head. Will she ever get used to a life where people felt it was okay to just walk up to someone and take their picture without permission, and to publish it without knowing the facts? She felt guilty for more than just inadvertently exposing him. She also had photos of him saved on her phone that she'd found either on the internet or on one or other social media account. A candid shot of him walking on a busy street with a set of earphones in his ears came to mind. Someone saw him, took a photo and posted it.

"As if he's public property," she fumed.

She'll never look at celebrity news the same ever again. She threw her phone on the couch. This was nothing she'd ever planned for and she didn't know how to deal with it.

Garridan will probably soon raise the question of her staying with him but she just wasn't sure. There was so much she needed to learn, to get used to. And she didn't think four days was enough time for her to make a proper decision. She wished she could go home for a while to clear her mind and then decide. But would Garridan be willing to wait for her?

Shelby paced the living room feeling more and more claustrophobic. She needed to vent, an outlet, but without Harlow, there was no one to speak to. This wasn't something she could speak to her mother about. She already knew what she'd say but her mother wouldn't be the one who'd have to live with the consequences of her decision if it went wrong.

The silence and waiting were oppressive, so Shelby decided to watch a movie. She turned on the TVand was relieved to find it already on a movie channel. She wanted to avoid celebrity gossip and anything that could remind her of their picture in the tabloids.

Thankfully, the movie playing was something she hadn't yet seen and it was only a few minutes in, so she could focus all her attention on it. She lost herself in one movie then another, and only realised the time when she heard the front door open.

"Hello?" Harlow called.

"In here," replied Shelby.

"Hey, Shel," Harlow greeted as she entered the living room. "You remember Rodrigo?"

Shelby looked away from the screen to greet the pair

and noticed their entwined fingers. She suddenly missed Garridan.

"Hi, guys. How was your morning?"

"It was great, thank you." Rodrigo said. His Spanish accent danced pleasantly around the English words.

In the brightness of the room, Shelby could see him clearer than when she first met him in the dimly-lit bar. He was very attractive with shoulder-length black hair, a deep golden skin tone, and hazel eyes that were framed by thick, long eyelashes. She could easily understand why Harlow was so taken by him.

"I'm glad you enjoyed it," Shelby smiled politely.

"What were you up to? What time did you get home?" Harlow asked.

Shelby wished she could tell Harlow about the picture but she didn't want to speak about it while Rodrigo was there.

"Garridan dropped me off late this morning and I didn't do anything much except watch some movies," she said, pointing to the TV.

"Are we still going shopping?" Harlow asked. "Is it okay if Rodrigo joins us?"

"Sure, I don't mind, if he doesn't mind walking around a mall looking for gifts with us."

Rodrigo lifted Harlow's hand to his lips and kissed her knuckles gently. "I'd love to," he said smoothly as he stared into her eyes.

Harlow giggled.

"Oh, and Garridan wants to take us to a show tomorrow night. Are you two down?" Shelby asked without explaining too much.

They exchanged looks as if in silent discussion and nodded. "Yeah, we're down," they said.

GARRIDAN

His talk show appearance went well. Garridan always enjoyed interacting with audiences and giving viewers insight to himself through discussions with the hosts. But he wasn't prepared when, while the cameras were rolling, one of the audience members asked if she could meet him personally after the show. Usually, a meet-and-greet was scheduled ahead of time and he could prepare for it. He didn't like being caught off guard and at first, he didn't know how to respond even though the show wasn't aired live. But eventually, because of the circumstances, he agreed.

Long after the show was recorded, he was still stuck at the studio chatting to some of the audience members who'd stayed behind. Garridan checked his watch and fidgeted in his chair.

Quincy shook his head from across the studio in silent reprimand.

Garridan glared in response. He was anxious to speak to Shelby. He worried that she'd be stressing about the picture and overthinking things, and he worried that it would be enough to convince her to say no. He desperately wanted to allay her fears and concerns, and especially her suggestion that she was somehow to blame for their picture ending up in the tabloids. Checking his watch again, he looked pleadingly at Quincy and Marc. He needed to get out of there. Soon.

When the last of the audience finally left, Garridan hurriedly greeted the host and rushed to his car, leaving Marc and Quincy behind. It was seven thirty-eight, still early enough for him to visit Shelby. As he drove towards her house, he briefly wondered if he should call ahead and ask if it was okay for him to come over, but he abandoned the thought when he remembered they were past the asking stage. When he finally arrived, he rang the doorbell and heard muffled talking from behind the door.

"Hi," Harlow greeted pleasantly as she opened the door. "She's in the living room. Go ahead."

Garridan entered the room and felt an instant wave of relief wash over him when he saw Shelby's face. He had no idea how much he'd missed her until he saw her. She didn't notice him at first because she was engrossed in the movie playing on the TV across the room. She sat on the couch, a plate with three slices of pizza balanced on her crossed legs.

"Hi," he said to no one in particular because there was a guy in the room too. He was seated on the floor next to the coffee table.

Looking up, Shelby pushed her plate aside and launched herself into Garridan's arms. He chuckled as he held her tightly, stroking her back. The guy on the floor cleared his throat and Shelby introduced them.

"Hey, it's good to meet you," Rodrigo said as they shook hands before turning his attention back to the TV.

Garridan followed Shelby to the couch.

Harlow returned to the room a few minutes later, carrying beers and handed one to each of the men. Garridan thanked her and took a slice of pizza from Shelby's plate. He relaxed into the cushions with her snuggling close to him, and he watched as Harlow and Rodrigo cuddled on the fluffy carpet at the coffee table. Garridan realised that he felt at ease for the first time since he dropped Shelby off that morning. And if he ever needed a reminder of what he wanted in his future, that moment right there was it.

Towards the middle of the movie, Shelby and Garridan excused themselves and went to her bedroom.

"This is a nice surprise," she said as she sat on the bed. She tapped the space beside her, beckoning him to sit.

He removed his jacket and shirt and placed them neatly on the chair in the corner. And only once he kicked off his shoes, did he take a seat next to her.

Shelby watched him closely; he looked stressed and his shoulders slumped. "How was the show?"

"Fun but tiring. We only left at seven thirty."

Shelby shook her head. "That's a really long day." Although she was interested in knowing about his appearance on the show, she could see he was tired, so she didn't ask for more details. "Did you eat?" she asked instead.

"Yeah, there were refreshments. And I had a slice of your pizza. Thank you." He smiled lazily.

"Massage?" she asked.

"Please."

It was the first time they'd had a moment like that but it felt as though they'd been doing it for years. She held his shoulders and coaxed him onto the bed. When he was comfortable, she straddled the back of his thighs and smoothed his undershirt. She started massaging his back rhythmically in slow, light movements to help him relax but his muscles were tense, so she applied pressure.

Garridan moaned.

"Do you wanna talk about it?" she asked after a few minutes.

"Not about work. I want to talk about you, about us."

She was expecting it, so she was prepared. "Alright," she agreed.

"Are you okay after the picture?"

She groaned inwardly. "I guess I'm okay now. I freaked out when you sent it to me because I feared you wouldn't want to see me again if it was my fault."

"So you accept that it's not your fault?" He lifted his head from the bed and waited for her to answer.

"I do feel partially responsible but when I think about it logically, people did recognise you earlier in the day even with your sunglasses on," she admitted.

"Good. So it's settled." His tone turned serious, "You know you'd have to get used to it if you decide to stay, right?"

She nodded even though he couldn't see her. "I realised that too because you said it happens all the time."

"How does it affect your decision?"

Shelby had been thinking about it all day. She was such a private person. She never posted anything on social media even though she was active on it all the time, she had a handful of friends, and never socialised. Apart from her professional website, even her career allowed her work to go public without drawing any attention to her. She did everything in her power to keep her personal life private. But a life with Garridan would lay it all bare to the world whether she wanted to or not. She wasn't sure she was ready for the limelight, much less being a topic of discussion. But she didn't know how to brace it with him.

When she didn't reply, Garridan turned around. She was still straddling him but this time, he faced her as he placed one hand on her thigh and the other arm under his head, waiting patiently.

"I want to say yes, but I don't know how I'll cope with all the attention," she said honestly. "Back home, I avoid attention. My privacy is sacred and I guard it as much as I possibly can. But with you, I won't have control over it."

He stared up at her waiting for her to finish.

"It's not that I have anything to hide. It's that I wouldn't want to embarrass my kids or you in any way. These vultures have a way of distorting everything and I wouldn't ever want to be a victim of a scandal, especially if it wasn't true."

Shelby hoped Garridan understood exactly what her fear was. He was very quiet and it looked as though he was giving it some thought.

"I agree that the media, the paparazzi and even the fans can be very ruthless and destructive," he said after a while. "But it's usually bred from speculation; if they see something unusual or something they're not sure of, they'll gossip about it. But if it's something people already know, it doesn't garner as much attention and it's labelled old news."

"That's true. No one wants to read about something they already know," Shelby agreed.

"So if I can find a way to protect you, to make you *old news*, will you stay?"

GARRIDAN

It was a long shot, but it was the only shot Garridan had. He'd do everything in his power to protect her if it meant she'd stay with him forever. His heart raced anxiously while he waited for her reply. He was terrified she wouldn't agree.

He joggled her impatiently and she laughed, breaking the tension. She recovered quickly, though, and as she studied him intently, he could almost hear her mind hard at work. The entire thing was nerve-racking.

When a slow smile crept across her face, he knew he was safe, but he held his breath as he waited for her to confirm it.

"Yes," she said.

Shelby couldn't believe her ears when she heard her own voice tell Garridan yes. But Garridan was on cloud nine. He whooped victoriously and lifted Shelby from his lap and laid her down, pinning her to the bed. He peppered her face with kisses and thanked her over and over again. He was like a child on Christmas morning. She was too stunned to move, to think, to react.

Did she really just agree to stay with him? Or did she agree to something else that made him ecstatically happy? Her thoughts were scrambled and her heart was racing a thousand kilometres per second. She was positive she'd pass out, but she breathed deeply and forced a smile.

After a few seconds of celebration, Garridan calmed down enough to hold her close. "Thank you," he said again and she could hear the relief in his voice.

"What for?" she asked, both as their usual response and to get confirmation of what exactly she'd agreed to.

"For agreeing to stay with me," he said happily, kissing her forehead. "I promise I'll protect you. You have nothing to worry about."

"How exactly will you protect me?" she asked curiously.

"Quincy is my PR Manager. I'll speak to him in the morning and we'll figure something out for the long term," he assured her. "But for now, it's all on me."

Garridan explained his intention to post some of the pictures they took at the beach on social media. That would eliminate speculation as to whether they were to-gether or not. He'd also tag her in the posts so that she wouldn't be labelled as 'unknown woman'. It would get attention initially, but would die down eventually.

Shelby shot up from the bed. "Garridan, my family will see those posts," she protested. "I haven't told them about us yet."

Garridan frowned. "When are you going to tell them?"

"I've only just decided to stay, so I haven't exactly thought about what comes after," she said in a panic. Everything was happening too quickly. It all felt so rushed. Shelby fanned her face. This time, she might definitely pass out.

He placed his hands calmly on her shoulders to placate her. "It's okay, babe. Don't worry. We'll wait until you're ready to tell them. But just remember that you're going to be seen with me, and more and more pictures will show up in the media," he reminded her. "You can't hide from it for-ever. And if you don't tell your family soon, you risk them finding out some other way."

Shelby nodded. Garridan was right, she couldn't risk her kids finding out about them on social media or TV. She had to tell them. Ideally, she would've told them when she went back home but because one photo had already surfaced from their time on a secluded section of a beach, she shuddered to think about what could happen when they partied it up the following night at an event packed to the brim with people.

She picked her phone up from the nightstand. "Do you wanna help me break the news?"

GARRIDAN

The video calls to Shelby's sons and parents went well. Garridan also had a chance to speak to them. Her older sons were young adults, so they supported her decision to pursue a relationship. All they wanted was for her to be happy and taken care of.

Her youngest son, Daniel, asked the most questions. He still lived at home with her and worried that he'd never see her again. But Shelby explained she would have to be home to make application and attend to various other things before she could come back to Garridan, and that perhaps he could join them when she was settled. He seemed sceptical but finally accepted her explanation.

"That wasn't so bad," she said after a while.

Garridan considered the discussions for a moment then asked, "Why did you think it wouldn't go well?"

"After their father, it was always only the four of us. I didn't have a proper relationship in all those years and the twins have never seen me with anyone other than him. Although, they were only two years old when he left, I doubt they remember." She looked thoughtful. "I tried, but I had my hands full with my job and raising the boys on my own, having a man in my life always felt like such a chore. I don't know if it was because they didn't understand the level of commitment single parenting required or because I just couldn't find someone I could connect with."

"So how long has it been?"

"The first time was when Daniel was nine and the last was six years ago, just before his thirteenth birthday. They were my only attempts and they were both very fleeting. The boys didn't even know about it."

"Why did you wait so long to try again?"

She sighed. "For a few reasons, actually, but the main one was that I didn't want to expose my sons to anyone who didn't intend on staying. And another, is judgement."

"Judgement?" Garridan asked. "Why would anyone judge you for trying to find love again?"

Shelby smiled and shook her head lightly. "When women who don't have kids fall in and out of relationships, people feel sorry for them. But when a single mother's relationships fail, people tend to blame her. They say she chose the wrong man because she's desperate or lonely. Can you believe that? We have the responsibility of caring for tiny human souls twenty-four seven and people think we're *lonely*. Sometimes, the only thing single parents crave is alone time. We pray for it."

"But your sons aren't little anymore. I'm sure someone eligible would've wanted your attention."

"I guess there were men who tried, but I wasn't really interested in filling my newly-acquired free time with a man. These last few years, I spent most of my time alone when I wasn't being a mom. My life is full and amazing. And besides," she nudged him playfully, "I had my hopes set on a certain out-of-reach celebrity."

"I'm glad you held out," he smiled.

"Me too," she said, leaning into him.

"But what's different between me and the other guys

you tried with?" he asked. Since he knew some of her story, he was curious to know what was different this time.

"The boys don't need me as much as they did before, so I can now focus on a relationship. Also, you already know I admired you for a long time. It's always been my dream to meet you even though the likelihood was less than zero, so when you stopped me in the street, it felt like fate was smiling down on me. I would never have let the opportunity of being with you slip away. New as it is, what we have is very different from my past experiences."

"And what's my rating thus far?" he asked, placing his fists on his sides like a superhero.

"I'm definitely not complaining," she laughed. "And what about you? How long has it been for you?"

He raised his eyebrows and sighed, contemplating his answer. "When I was younger, I dated some of my co-stars. I guess when we're acting, we pour so much of ourselves into the characters that we develop feelings through them. The relationships tended to last a few weeks after filming or while we promoted the movie. But once we moved on to the next thing, the feelings faded. It was all very fleeting as you said, and after a while it got old. So I don't do that anymore. I've had brief relationships recently but they didn't amount to much."

"Do you still develop feelings for your co-stars?" she asked and Garridan could hear the concern in her voice.

"I always keep things professional and I've learnt to divorce my personal self from the actor. Occasionally, someone tries to start a relationship with me but I let them down nicely. I keep it purely professional. For the most part, I develop friendships." He couldn't read her expression. "What have you heard?"

"I don't stalk you online if that's what you're asking, so I didn't know about your co-stars. And none of your posts were about your relationships. But I read once that someone tried to set you up with Jasmin Raj but she was already secretly dating Billy Wolff."

"Yeah, that actually happened," Garridan chuckled as his mind wandered to the breathtaking, recently-married A-list couple – the Hindu beauty and her multi-talented singer-actor husband.

Shelby's eyes grew wide and her jaw dropped. "Garridan, I'll never be able to compete with that level of beauty and fame!" She looked down at herself. "There's nothing remarkable about me. Why would you even want to be with me when you have supermodel-types throwing themselves at you? I don't fit into your world. It all makes me feel very insecure." She looked defeated as she folded her arms across her chest.

He pulled her into his arms. He understood her concerns but he also knew his feelings for her, and they grew stronger the more time he spent with her. Not like when he was in character, but in real life. His true self was falling for her. He knew that nothing he'd say would alleviate her insecurities but he planned on showing her everyday how serious he was about her and he hoped it would be enough.

"Baby, you don't have to compete with anyone. I wish you could see yourself through my eyes, then you'd know why I feel the way I do about you. The world you speak of is just me putting on different faces as and when it needs me to. You get the true me – the one who wants you more than anything. I don't ever want you to doubt my feelings for you or how much you mean to me, okay?"

"Okay," she nodded.

A soft knock on the door drew their attention.

"Come in," Shelby answered.

Harlow entered the room to tell them that Rodrigo was leaving, so they headed to the living room to quickly discuss their plans for the Fourth. Garridan and Rodrigo took charge and finalised the arrangements while Shelby and Harlow listened. They exchanged goodnights and Harlow walked with Rodrigo to his car.

Shelby started gathering the empty bottles and pizza boxes that littered the living room. Garridan helped her and carried the things he'd picked up to the kitchen. He was beat. He had a long and emotional day and all he wanted was to crawl into bed and sleep. No, he wanted to crawl into Shelby's bed and sleep with her in his arms.

When she entered the kitchen behind him, he leaned against the counter and held her close, wrapping his arms lightly around her waist. She curled her arms around his neck and looked up at him. Garridan could see the adoration in her eyes. No one's ever looked at him like that. Her hair was in a messy bun atop her head, and in an old t-shirt and shorts, she looked so carefree and innocent. His growing feelings for her made him feel vulnerable.

"Can I stay with you tonight?" he croaked as he settled his forehead against hers.

She simply smiled and nodded before she led him to her room.

As Garridan followed behind her, Shelby was a ball of nerves. She couldn't understand why she felt that way because they'd shared a bed just the night before. Somehow this time felt different. It meant more. She fought so hard to contain her feelings for him, but the more time she spent with him, the deeper she fell.

When she crawled into bed next to him, Garridan pulled her into his side. They lay in the dark, speaking about what their life together would be like, and before long, they were both fast asleep.

The following morning, Shelby woke to the aroma of coffee and pancakes. Garridan's spot was empty and she wondered how long he'd been up. She padded to the bathroom before searching for him. She found him in the kitchen standing in front of a mountain of pancakes.

"Good morning," he greeted her pleasantly. He looked relaxed and fresh and his blue eyes sparkled.

"Good morning," she smiled, looking around. "What are you doing?" she asked as she sat on a barstool across the counter from him.

"Making breakfast of course," he said, stating the obvious. "It's your first Independence Day here and I want it to be memorable." He placed a plateful of pancakes and a mug of coffee in front of her and hugged her from behind, placing sweet kisses in her neck. "Happy Fourth, baby."

Shelby all but melted. Garridan had surprised her every day since they'd met. His sweet, thoughtful nature and his adorable ways made her fall for a new side of him each time. The day she'd been looking forward to for so long hadn't even started yet and it was already amazing.

She turned in her chair and hugged him around his waist, her head pressed against his heart. "Happy Independence Day, Garridan. Thank you so much. I already love it."

Harlow joined them later and the three of them enjoyed breakfast together. Garridan left shortly afterwards to get ready for a fundraising event he'd be attending that afternoon, and promised he'd be back later for their night out. Shelby walked with him to his car and when he closed his door, she leaned into the window to give him a passionate kiss goodbye.

"Check your phone," he said mischievously.

When she returned to the house, Harlow was squealing, jumping up and down in the kitchen. She held her phone out and shook it in Shelby's face. It looked as though she wanted to say something but was dumbstruck by whatever had caught her attention. The only words she could muster were "Omigod! Omigod! Omigod!" while she waved her hands excitedly.

Shelby shook her head and pried the phone from Harlow's hand. But what she saw astounded her. There, on the screen, was a picture of her and Garridan. It was a social media post from Garridan's public account which she was tagged in. The photo was one from their date at the beach where he reclined between her legs and she held him from behind, resting her chin on his shoulder. Their hands were laced together on her knee and they smiled brightly. It was one of her favourite photos. The caption read: *Here's to the first of many with my love, Shelby #happyindependenceday*

She couldn't stop looking at it. Once again, Garridan managed to leave her breathless. He'd posted it more than an hour earlier, and it garnered hundreds of thousands of likes and thousands of comments. She wished she'd known about it earlier because she would've liked to be one of the first to comment.

On her own phone, she liked the post and read some of the comments. Her phone was abuzz with incoming messages from friends and family back home who'd also seen the post. They wanted to know everything.

One of the messages was from Garridan. *Your turn*, it read. Shelby bit her lip nervously, knowing he meant it was her turn to post something. The night before, she reluctantly agreed to post something too, but she didn't know she'd have to do it in the aftermath of his breaking news.

She asked Harlow for help.

"Which one do you think I should post?" she asked, showing Harlow the photos Garridan had sent her.

Harlow looked through them thoughtfully and squealed again when she saw one with them laughing at something. "Definitely this one!"

Shelby studied the photo: she was lying on her back, resting her head on Garridan's thigh. He held up her hand, curling his fingers around hers. She looked up at him and he was looking down at her. They were laughing as if they shared a private joke. In the background, two seagulls flew overhead against the striking blue sky. It looked as though someone else had captured the moment while lying in the sand next to them.

"Who took this picture?" Harlow asked, making the same observation.

"I did. We pretended to be our own paparazzi," she recalled with a giggle.

"It's a stunning photo. You should post it."

Inhaling deeply, Shelby mustered up the courage to send her first ever PDA post. She tagged Garridan's public account and captioned the photo: *One of my favourite moments. Happy Independence Day, my love*

She silenced the ringer and locked her phone because it was now alive with reactions and comments.

Harlow smiled and said, "Congratulations! You're officially famous!" She then laughed uncontrollably.

Shelby simply rolled her eyes before she collapsed onto the couch and joined Harlow in a fit of laughter.

For the rest of the morning, they spent girl-time prepping their outfits for their date with Garridan and Rodrigo. The compulsory colour theme was red, white and blue, so they made sure they had what they needed before enjoying the holiday outside with the rest of America.

They were real tourists, taking lots of photos and selfies, making the most of the holiday. They were each responsible for choosing an activity and Shelby's choice was an all-American Fourth of July barbeque at one of the local hotels. The atmosphere was fun and patriotic, and Shelby enjoyed the camaraderie and stories shared around the grill.

Later on, they embarked on Harlow's choice of adventure – barhopping along a lengthy sidewalk packed with little cafés, tasting different cocktails. It was Harlow's idea of loosening up for their date with the guys and quashing nerves before the job interviews she had lined up for the following afternoon.

By the time they returned to their house, they were ready for an evening that promised to surpass either of their expectations.

GARRIDAN

After a quick shower, Garridan was ready to leave for the night. The fundraiser was a huge success and he was in the mood to celebrate. He was also eager to see Shelby and tell her about his day. Before he left, he cast an appraising eye around the room and smiled as he slipped a small box into his pocket.

On the drive over, an edginess crept into Garridan as he recalled Shelby's aversion to attention. It would be their first public appearance together and he didn't know what to expect. Because of the show's line-up, journalists would be in attendance to report on the event and he hoped they'd be too preoccupied with the performing artists than to care about his date. He wiped a sweaty hand across his jeans and took a deep breath. Hopefully the night would be uneventful. The last thing he needed was for his day that started off so amazingly, to be ruined by pushy reporters.

Rodrigo opened the door at Shelby's place and invited Garridan in. The ladies were busy with last-minute finishing touches, so Garridan and Rodrigo got acquainted with each other while they waited. Garridan was surprised to learn that, in his youth, Rodrigo was a talented football player and had scouts lining up to draft him, but his hopes of playing professionally were shattered when he suffered a serious injury during a homecoming game.

"That's crazy, man. I'm sorry," Garridan said. He

couldn't imagine what it must've been like to have something so close within reach only to lose it to an accident.

"Thanks," Rodrigo said sadly. "But it all worked out in the end. I'm head coach at my old high school now. And it's really fulfilling working with the kids."

The clicking of heels drew their attention to the passage leading from the bedrooms to the living room. They stood in anticipation and smiled when Harlow walked in. She looked pretty in white jeans, a glittery blue top and stilettos. Her makeup was bold and her usually curly hair was straightened and slicked to hang over her one shoulder. The gleam in Rodrigo's eyes when he looked at her, resembled the sparkle of her top.

"You look gorgeous," Rodrigo said and Harlow's cheeks flushed as she smiled up at him.

They excused themselves and went to the kitchen to get some drinks, leaving Garridan alone in the living room. A few minutes later, another set of heels clicked down the passage. Garridan stood expectantly and waited for his beauty to arrive and when she did, she took his breath away.

The stunning crimson dress she wore kissed the top of her knees. It dipped dangerously low in front, and swept along the slant of her waist and glided around the arch of her hips. Its long sleeves offset the dress' revealing feel. Dramatic makeup made her eyes smoulder and her lips even more alluring. Her long hair was also straightened; its sides slicked and pinned back with a pretty clip.

"You're so beautiful," he said in a low voice before he pecked her forehead. He hoped his tone would convey just how drawn he was to her in that moment. His physical attraction to Shelby was hard to suppress on a normal day, but he knew it would be nearly impossible now. He also knew he wouldn't be able to take his eyes off her even if he tried.

"Thank you," she said. "I wanted to try on glamorous for a change," she added playfully as she twirled, looking comfortable in her four-inch stilettos.

Garridan grinned. "It looks damn good on you."

Shelby stood back and studied him. Her eyes did not hide her emotions when they widened slightly as she took him in. "You look amazing too," she said with a lilt in her voice that sounded the way it did when he kissed her.

Garridan had the sudden urge to call off their plans and spend the rest of the night in her bedroom. Thankfully, Harlow and Rodrigo returned from the kitchen. Rodrigo carried a small tray with four shot glasses and held it out for each of them to take one. He put the tray on the table, pulled Harlow into his side, and raised his glass to make a toast.

"Here's hoping we get to spend many more amazing days with you ladies. Salud!"

"Cheers!" Harlow, Shelby and Garridan shouted in chorus.

They clinked glasses and downed the shot before heading out.

The queue outside the club was long but Garridan only had to greet the bouncer and they were in. Inside, Shelby struggled to get used to the bright, strobing lights. When her eyes finally adjusted, she noticed how incredible the venue was. Garridan held her hand as they wove between the patrons. Every now and then, someone would call his name and he'd greet with a nod or a smile.

"Do you know any of them," she asked curiously over the loud music.

He shook his head.

The hostess spotted Garridan and led them to an empty table close to the stage. Once they were settled, Shelby could take a better look around. She noticed the unique décor and the theatrical setup which made it feel more like a celebrity awards event than a club.

Rodrigo ordered bottles of whiskey and cranberry vodka. Shelby hesitated when a drink was placed on the table in front of her. She frowned at the thought of how much alcohol she'd already had for the day, after the cocktails with Harlow, and Rodrigo's shooters earlier.

Garridan leaned in. "What's wrong?" he asked.

She shook her head not wanting to be a buzzkill. But Garridan insisted.

"It's too much alcohol for me," she said and told him about the other drinks she'd had before the one at home.

He nodded and gestured that he'd be back and left

their table. A few minutes later, he returned with bottles of water. He opened one and handed it to Shelby. She thanked him and drank thirstily on the cold liquid. Garridan watched her closely and looked satisfied when she had enough to keep her hydrated.

The venue was still fairly empty and the atmosphere was light, expectant. They sat in comfortable silence taking in the scene around them and chatting occasionally about random things. But as more people arrived, the atmosphere shifted to one of a celebration. People were laughing and dancing, and just generally having fun. The constant droning of the bass vibrated through Shelby, beating life into her. Their little group also became livelier.

When the thumping beat of a popular reggaeton song boomed through the speakers, Harlow and Rodrigo jumped up and sang along loudly. She started dancing and he surprised her by taking her hand, leading their steps in an authentic Latin rhythm. They looked good together.

Shelby looked over at Garridan who cocked an eyebrow as if to say 'don't even think about asking me to dance' and she laughed out loud. But his hesitation didn't stop her. She stood in front of him and danced in perfect harmony with the music. Closing her eyes and pretending he was her dance partner, she swayed her hips and allowed her body to flow naturally with the rhythm. The lyrics spurred her on. Dancing for Garridan was a heady experience, so she gave him a performance she hoped he'd never forget.

When the song was over, Shelby opened her eyes and looked at Garridan. His wide gaze was fixed on her and he wiped a hand across his mouth. His stunned expression was priceless and so adorable, she couldn't help but laugh. He was speechless but the fire in the depths of his eyes said more than words ever could. And when she sat, he pulled her into him and kissed her deeply, apparently not caring that they had an audience.

When he pulled back, he said, "Do that again, and we'll have to leave early." He waggled his eyebrows and she laughed again.

He eventually did dance with them but on condition it was on the dance floor. They agreed and used the space just outside the area they were seated in.

As expected, people often interrupted them to speak to Garridan or to take a photo. Some of the reporters who attended the event also stopped by and took a group shot of Garridan and his guests, and Shelby appreciated how professional they were. But she was pleasantly surprised when two young women came up to her and asked if she was the Shelby he'd posted about that morning and when she said yes, they squealed and told her they loved her. It was Garridan's turn to laugh at her reaction.

The show itself was incredible and watching it from the proximity of their table was an exhilarating experience. Popular bands performed in honour of soldiers stationed in war-torn countries, and the proceeds were for a foundation that provided support to families whose loved ones had died or gone missing in combat. Apart from the bands that performed, other celebrities attended the event too – actors, singers, rappers – and Garridan introduced them when they came to their table to say hi. Shelby had to admit she felt a little star-struck more than once. And from the look on Harlow and Rodrigo's faces, they'd probably agree with her.

When Harlow and Rodrigo decided to explore the club and join in on the festivities with the younger crowd, Shelby scooted into Garridan's side. He kissed her temple and they chatted as much as they could over the noise. She asked about the fundraiser and he excitedly told her about its massive success and how many children's lives would change because of the donations they'd received. She told him how proud she was of him and that she was excited to get involved when she came back. That earned her another passionate kiss. When the kiss ended, he reached into his pocket and pulled out a black velvet box and placed it in her hand. She looked at him questioningly.

"Open it," he said.

Shelby opened the box carefully and gasped, her hand clamped over her mouth when she saw what it held. She couldn't contain her joy. Garridan reached over and gently pulled the delicate necklace out of the box. He gestured for her to turn and when she did, he clasped it around her neck.

She stared at it in wonder. On their date at the beach, she told him about a necklace she'd once seen in an advertisement and wanted to buy, but it was only available in the USA. She was again disappointed when she found out as soon as she arrived in the U.S., that it was sold out. Garridan said he'd try to find one for her but she didn't think he'd actually buy it. He was so thoughtful and caring, and everything he did made her feel loved and appreciated. She wasn't used to being lavished that way. And it wasn't the material value, it was the depth of Garridan's affection for her.

"You shouldn't have," she said after a while.

He shook his head. "I wanted you to have something to remember me by if you decided to never come back." He lowered his gaze as if the thought pained him.

"It's beautiful, Garridan. I love it. Thank you so much," she mouthed because the words were stuck in her throat.

He kissed her forehead. "You're welcome," he said and then he described the detail.

The one she wanted was a dark, spherical pendant speckled with stars which reminded Shelby of a mystical planet lightyears away. But Garridan had hers customised to contain the phrase 'I love you' in English, Romanian and Afrikaans. The words were only visible when the pendant was held up to the light. He also added their names.

Shelby couldn't see it in the club's lighting but she already knew she loved it by his description. She flung her arms around his neck and thanked him again.

"Anything to make you happy," he smiled.

Sometime later, Garridan asked, "Will you be okay on your own for a few minutes?"

Shelby nodded. She didn't think Harlow and Rodrigo would be back anytime soon.

While he was gone, she looked out over the sea of people around her, watching them interact with each other. She spotted Harlow and Rodrigo with a group across the dance floor and they looked like they were having the best time. She was still deep in thought about the gift Garridan had given her and about how blessed she was, when someone tapped her shoulder. She turned with a smile expecting Garridan but instead, there were two women glaring down at her. Their aggressive stance caused Shelby to reflexively lean back in her seat. She frowned as she studied them, trying to gauge their intentions.

The blonde's white dress hugged every inch of her voluptuous body. With her long, fake lashes and blunt bob, she reminded Shelby of one of those models who looked like they were mass-produced in a factory. In a blue and gold asymmetric skirt and matching crop top, the brunette was just as curvaceous as her friend. Shelby stood because the pair staring down at her was intimidating. But even in her high heels, they towered a head taller than her.

"Can I help you?" she asked. "Are you looking for Garridan?"

The blonde grimaced and scowled at Shelby. "Garridan is mine, bitch!" she said with absolute venom in her tone. "I don't know who you think you are and what you think you're doing, you gold-digging whore. Stay away from him or I'll make your life a living hell."

Shelby flinched even though the woman didn't touch her. She'd never even considered the perception her relationship with Garridan would have created, so the verbal assault was worse than a slap across the face. But she quickly recovered. She had no idea who this woman was and why she felt she had a claim on Garridan, but Shelby had to avoid a scene at all costs. As much as she could hold her own, she had to remember where she was.

"Look, I don't know who you are," she said without inflection, while working hard to maintain her composure. "But, if you have a problem with my relationship with Garridan, I suggest you get used to it because I'm not going anywhere."

The brunette stepped between them, bending forward to look Shelby straight in the eye. "Tell him he's going to be a daddy," she said spitefully.

Shelby flinched for a second time.

"What's going on here?" Garridan asked from behind the two women, startling them and Shelby.

In the heat of their confrontation, none of them noticed his return.

Garridan stood closer and Shelby noticed a deep crease in his brow. "Are you okay?" he asked, reaching for her hand.

She placed her hand in his and nodded.

"What do you want, Kimber?" he asked.

The blonde shot Shelby one last look of disgust before she faced Garridan. "Ask your little gold digger," she said as she stalked past him, knocking his shoulder in the process.

GARRIDAN

Garridan ran a hand through his hair and tugged on the ends. Shelby was clearly upset by the confrontation with Kimber but she didn't want to speak about it.

"Let's just pretend it didn't happen, okay?" she said with a sad expression. She glanced over his shoulder. "People are watching. Let's not give them something to gossip about," she added, smiling brightly.

But Garridan knew it was all a show because his heart didn't flutter like it did with her real smile. He sighed and followed suit, slipping on a mask of happiness and relying heavily on his acting skills to carry him through the rest of the night. He and Shelby co-stars on a stage. They acted as though nothing was wrong – laughing, dancing, little kisses here and there – even he was nearly fooled by their performance. Nearly. Until he caught the sad, distant look in her eye.

By the time Harlow and Rodrigo returned to their table, Garridan was ready to leave. Most of the patrons had already left and only those who were very drunk, very lonely or very in love remained. Garridan absently wondered which category he belonged to.

The drive home was quiet, strained even. Harlow and Rodrigo cuddled in the backseat and when Garridan caught a glimpse of them in the rearview mirror, they seemed more intimate than before. Their growing feelings for each other were obvious. Garridan smiled. Knowing

Harlow's reason for coming to Miami, he was happy she'd found someone she connected with.

Shelby held his hand and sat just as close as usual but she felt miles away. She watched the road and occasionally glanced at him. She smiled but it was a sad smile. His heart pinched when he saw it but instantly started beating rapidly. What if she changed her mind?

He looked at her questioningly, hoping she'd give him a sign that everything between them was still okay. "Tired?" he asked.

She shook her head. "Not really."

"Will you come to the hotel with me?" He was desperately clinging to hope.

"Yes."

Garridan released the breath he was holding.

"Can I grab some stuff first?" she asked.

"Of course."

She sighed and leaned her head against the window, looking wistfully at the beach they were passing. Garridan realised it was where they'd spent the most amazing day together. It'd been only two days since their first date but it felt like a lifetime ago. So much had happened since then, so many bonds had been formed, emotions confessed, promises made and, now, a rift.

Garridan was determined to get to the bottom of it. He wasn't going to allow Shelby to bury whatever had transpired between her and Kimber. He couldn't allow his past to drive a wedge between them. What could Kimber possibly have said that caused this kind of reaction, this level of detachment? He couldn't think of anything he might have done. Shelby knew he'd dated recently and that nothing had come of it. Granted, he didn't tell her *who* he'd dated, but she must've seen photos of them in the tabloids or in celebrity news at some point. Kimber always made sure they were pictured together.

His time with Kimber was tumultuous, to say the least. She was sweet in the beginning and they seemed to get along, but the relationship slowly morphed into something of a bad reality TV show. Although they'd only spent a few weeks together, most of it was ruined by drama and insecurity on her part. Garridan tried to be patient with her and gave her everything she wanted, but nothing he did was good enough. She wanted marriage, she wanted fame and she demanded extravagant displays of affection, always acting out and wanting attention at the most inopportune times. The more he gave of himself, the more she demanded.

He wasn't ready for what she wanted. And he especially wasn't interested in continuing a relationship with someone as self-absorbed and toxic as Kimber, so he called it off. He hadn't heard from her for at least three months.

Shelby could sense Garridan's unease. She knew it was unfair to distance herself from him, even if just a little. It was also unfair to not say anything about the altercation in the club. He desperately wanted to know because he wanted to fix it. But this wasn't something he could fix.

She didn't blame him; she blamed herself. She knew she didn't fit into his world. She knew she wasn't as glamorous and beautiful as the women he was used to. She knew there'd be drama. And she knew she wouldn't give him a child. She knew all that but still she allowed herself to be sucked into a relationship with him. Now, all her fears were manifested in one night – the drama, the gorgeous ex, the baby. Shelby couldn't compete. Garridan and everything that came with him were way out of her league. And just like that, her fantasy disintegrated before her eyes.

She looked over at Garridan. He was so beautiful, even in profile. His eyes were still bright despite how late it was, but she noticed worry lines around them that weren't there before. Probably a testament of the weariness he felt. His full lips were drawn down, making him look sad. Is that what he was feeling? He hadn't let go of her hand since they'd gotten into the car. Shelby felt like his anchor. It puzzled her. It also enraged her. Garridan's emotional state and his entire demeanour cast him as the victim when, in fact, she should be the one acting that way. She felt an urge to pry her hand from his but fought it and swallowed against the knot that started to form in her throat.

There were so many questions but she knew that even if she had the answers, it wouldn't change the fact that this dark cloud in the shape of a blonde bombshell and her love child would hang over their heads forever. Why did she say he was hers? Was she really carrying his baby? Did she live in Miami? Did he know she was there? Did he love her at some point? Will he take her back for the sake of the baby? Her mind was a battlefield and her head pounded from all the uncertainty. All she wanted to do was go home to South Africa where everything was familiar and pre-dictable and boring.

When Garridan finally stopped in her driveway, she snatched her hand from his to open the door, and let go of a breath she didn't know she was holding.

GARRIDAN

Garridan waited in the car, too afraid to walk into the house with Shelby. He was afraid of what he'd see in her eyes in the bright light of her bedroom. He was terrified that, if he went inside, she wouldn't want to go back to the hotel with him. He felt like a coward but he wasn't ready to face the possibility of losing her.

For the hundredth time that night, he breathed a sigh of relief. Shelby was walking out of the house towards his car carrying a backpack. She was going with him after all. He still had hope.

The drive to the hotel was tenser than before. With only them in the car, their ruse was no longer necessary. Garridan was torn between giving her the space she so obviously wanted, and satisfying his own need for her touch. His desire to always please her won. Soon they'd be in his hotel room and they'd put this misunderstanding behind them and everything would be right again.

The hotel lobby was quiet but given the time, it was expected. Some of the staff greeted them politely as they made their way to the elevators, and Shelby vaguely wondered how many women Garridan had brought here before her.

After the incident in the club, it was clear she didn't know him at all. How could she ever think it would work between them? She was naïve. Just because he didn't post about women, it didn't mean he wasn't seeing them. Maybe they got a special mention on his private accounts. What if she was just one more of many women he was already dating?

Garridan held her hand as they entered the elevator. She allowed him to because as much as she hated to admit it, she needed his touch now more than ever. She'd been hurt before. Plenty of times. But she always bounced back soon after and wrote the episode off as life experience. This time, however, she wasn't so sure. She never let anyone get as close to her as she allowed Garridan to. She was never as vulnerable as she was with him. What she felt this time was more than hurt.

She knew that when they got to his room, he'd want to talk. She wished she could avoid it all because it wouldn't make a difference. But she also knew she'd have to be mature about it and now that she'd had some time to think and process everything, she was prepared.

His room was on the eighteenth floor. As they walked down the long corridor, it occurred to Shelby that she'd never expected him to reserve the penthouse like movies depict celebrities do. He was too humble to do something like that. She smiled when she realised she'd just compared Garridan's life to a movie.

When they reached his room, he hesitated at the door and looked over at her. She thought he was going to say something but he simply pursed his lips and swiped the key card to unlock the door, swinging it open for her to enter before him.

It was a suite. Shelby's jaw dropped and her hands flew to her face, cupping her cheeks. On the floor, hundreds of red rose petals created a path from the door into the spacious living room area. It continued across the room, down the hallway and disappeared around a soft bend. Tall candles burnt on the mantel, the coffee table and other smaller tables that occupied the room, casting a soothing glow. Slow RnB music played softly from the stereo in the corner and there was a hint of vanilla in the air.

She kicked off her shoes and stepped tentatively onto the petal path. It was soft and velvety beneath her bare feet. She followed the path into the living room and stopped at the candle on the coffee table, running her fingers around the smooth top. It was scented and she tried to recall when she told Garridan she loved vanilla. She followed the candles around the room, taking in every detail around her.

When she was done, Garridan held her hand and led her down the petal path into the hallway. The passage was short and the curve brought her to the entrance of a stunning bedroom. The path continued to the king size bed in the middle of the room. There, more rose petals were scattered across the bed and just like in the living room, vanilla-scented candles cast a glow which now felt more sensual as the slow, soft music wafted through the speakers in the walls.

Shelby raised her arms and twirled giddily in circles before falling backwards onto the bed, causing the petals to launch into the air. She giggled with delight as the petals rained down on her.

She was in ecstasy. No one has ever made her feel as loved and as special as Garridan has in those few days. That was exactly why she was falling in love with him.

Garridan watched as Shelby enjoyed her surprise. It was their second last night in Miami and he wanted to do something special for her. She was so sweet and caring and selfless, he got the feeling she didn't usually get spoilt. He wanted her to know just how deeply he cared for her.

She lay on the bed, her arms spread above her head and her legs dangling over the side. She stared at the ceiling with a beautiful smile on her face. Garridan's heart fluttered. That smile was real.

He approached the bed carefully, still not sure if things between them were fine. The surprise may have temporarily pulled her out of her sullen mood but he didn't want to make assumptions. He didn't want to risk anything. As he reached the bed and looked down at her, she turned her head and stared at him.

"Kiss me," she whispered.

Her words were so soft, Garridan thought he imagined them, but the undeniable love in her gaze told him he didn't. He leaned down and claimed her mouth. She tasted of cranberry vodka and it had a dizzying effect as she kissed him back hungrily. He couldn't believe he was there with her like that. He couldn't believe how the universe had sewed pieces together in a way that brought them to each other. He'd waited for her all his life and wanted to prove to her just how much he needed and wanted her.

He paced their kiss and slowed the tempo. He didn't want to rush; he wanted to cherish every moment. He lifted her from the bed while the sultry vocalist sang overhead. Garridan's movements were slow but sure. They danced to the soulful music and he took control, wanting Shelby to forget. Wanting to relieve her of any doubt of his feelings for her. The smooth lyrics caressed them and as the rhythm climaxed, Garridan couldn't restrain himself anymore. He claimed her. Worshipped her body. Taking his time and revelling in the feel of her softness against him. Every touch, a blessing. Every kiss, a prayer. Every moan from her sweet mouth, a declaration. No one has ever made him feel so raw, so exposed, so whole. As he took her to the brink, she proclaimed her undying love for him. The holy grail. He followed soon after with a declaration of his own, cleaving his soul to hers in ecstatic union.

They lay facing each other in the middle of the bed, fingers entwined between them. They'd been lying that way for hours, enveloped in the afterglow of their lovemaking. The rising sun peeked through the bedroom window, casting shadows across Garridan's handsome face. His eyes were bright, clear as the morning sky and they were staring at her intently. Shelby stared into their crystal depths and wondered what he saw when he looked at her that way. She tried to decipher it – love, passion, devotion, she finally decided because that's what it felt like.

It was their last day in Miami. Her last day in the United States. Soon they'd be continents apart. With an ache in her heart, she wondered if the distance would change things between them. She knew that when she got back home, she'd fall back into her routine – work and family. Her life would go back to normal while she waited for the arrangements for her return to Garridan to be finalised. He had nothing to worry about because there was nothing and no one back home that threatened her commitment to him.

But what about him? How will his return to Los Angeles affect him? Will he simply carry on where he left off or will he make changes for her return? Will he continue to date casually while he waited? Will he speak to Kimber and find an amicable solution?

They'd discussed the previous night's drama and he assured her that Kimber was a thing of the past, that he hadn't seen her in months and he promised he'd make things right. But even after his assurances, her doubts ran deep. The possibility of losing him was all too real.

"What are you thinking?" he asked suddenly, pulling her from her thoughts.

"Will you wait for me?"

He drew closer to her and their bodies meshed together. "I've been waiting for you. For so long," he said earnestly. "I don't know what I'm going to do without you."

"I'm scared." Rebellious tears threatened to spill over her lashes.

"Of what?" he asked.

The weight of her questions was wearing her down. If Garridan was serious about her, she'd have to trust he'd welcome and appreciate her honesty.

"I'm scared you'll get tired of waiting and you'll move on. Date. Fix things with Kimber in a way that will make you hers. Stuff like that."

He placed a gentle hand on her cheek and brushed a wayward tear with his thumb. "You're the one I want. I need you. No matter how long it takes, I'll be waiting for only you. I know it's been just a few days but I love you, baby. Please believe me."

She nodded. "And I love you," she said. It was all she could muster.

GARRIDAN

"I'll see you at around seven thirty," Garridan said. He was resting against his car in front of Shelby's house, his arms locked around her waist as she leaned against him.

She looked up at him adoringly. He loved it when she did that.

"Okay. I'll be here," she said.

He was reluctant to leave. Deep down, he wished he didn't have to attend the on-air interview at the radio station but it was important. He always showed up, no matter what.

"You know I would've stayed, right?"

She nodded. "I know that. But I also know how important your career is. I wouldn't have been able to love you like I do if you were negligent about your commitment to it."

He squatted and lifted her from the ground and cradled her to him. "God you're amazing! And I'm going to miss the hell out of you today," he said, playfully giving her Eskimo kisses.

"I'm gonna miss you too," she giggled as he lowered her to the ground. "Is there anything you want when you come back?"

He grinned slyly and cocked an eyebrow.

"Not that!" she laughed. "I meant to eat or drink or do."

"No, thank you. I just want to spend the rest of the night with you."

"That can be arranged. Now off you go," she said as she turned him around and swatted his butt.

He laughed, shaking his head as he got into his car and started it. Shelby poked her head through the window and kissed him quickly before he drove off.

Shelby checked her watch again. Ten twenty-three. She'd been pacing for hours; an ominous feeling clawing at her. Rodrigo and Harlow were visiting in the living room. He wanted to spend her last night in the country with her, and they were also celebrating a job offer she'd received. Shelby stayed put in the kitchen, too distracted to be good company.

"Are you sure he said seven thirty tonight?" Harlow asked when she came into the kitchen for more beers. "What if he meant tomorrow morning?"

Shelby glared at her cousin. "We would have boarded the plane by then," she said, not bothering to hide her irritation.

Harlow shrugged and returned to the living room where Rodrigo was waiting for her.

The pacing continued. Shelby had sent several messages and tried to call Garridan but it went straight to voicemail. It was so unusual because she was always able to get hold of him. Apart from that, she'd grown accustomed to the messages he'd send even on his busiest days, but she hadn't received even one since he left that afternoon.

Her heart raced as a dark thought crossed her mind and she went into the living room, too freaked out to be alone. "What if something happened to him?" she asked Harlow.

Harlow shook her head. "Marc or Quincy would've

called you," she reasoned. "Or even Megan," she added as an afterthought.

"But they all work together and attend everything together. What if something happened to all of them? No-one else knows me, so they wouldn't think of calling me if anything happened to him." She chewed her fingernail and peered out of the window.

"We've already checked the news headlines. There was nothing about him," said Rodrigo.

"Except those cute damn photos of you dancing for him in the club that everyone keeps talking about," Harlow added, rolling her eyes.

That wasn't enough to comfort Shelby. "Can you check again, please? I'm sorry to ask but I'm really worried and I can't focus long enough to do it myself."

Her imagination was running away with her. She conjured up many scenarios of what could possibly have gone wrong, most of them ending with Garridan being hurt. She didn't want to think anymore. Because the thought that kept nudging at her was the one she was most desperately trying to avoid. The one that included Kimber.

"Are you sure he said he'll be at a radio *interview*?" Harlow asked, emphasising the word.

"Of course. Why?"

"Because I'm looking at a picture posted by Kimber Allyn. She tagged Garridan." Harlow handed her phone to Shelby with sympathy in her eyes. "It looks like a massive party. I'm sorry, Shel."

Shelby stared at the phone in stunned silence. Three things struck her at once. First, Kimber Allyn was Garridan's supposedly pregnant ex. Second, she was at an event that he was apparently attending. And third, could Kimber be the reason he was still at the 'interview' instead of with her? She looked at the picture again. It wasn't a selfie. Someone had taken the photo of Kimber dancing; head flung back, eyes closed as if lost in the music and hands pointing to the sky. It captured the scene behind her too. The crowd appeared to be having a great time as they danced with smiling faces, holding bottles in the air. Did Garridan take this photo?

Shelby tried hard not to speculate because she knew how dangerous and unfair it was. But what other option did she have when he was acting out of character? Garridan has always been reliable. He was prompt and he was trustworthy. He'd always let her know if he was running late. But with Kimber's sudden appearance, his silence could only mean one thing.

She thanked Harlow politely and made an excuse to leave the room. She went to her bedroom and sat pensively on her bed. Nausea churned her stomach and she suppressed the urge to vomit. She wrapped her arms tightly around her waist and squeezed, hoping the nausea would subside. Tears pricked her eyes and all of a sudden, she was transported back nineteen years. Déjà vu. History was repeating itself. All the clichés.

Shelby didn't know how to feel. The nausea was replaced by rage, disappointment substituted tears, and the hurt turned to humiliation. Is this what a life with Garridan would be like? Constant doubt and ghosts from the past haunting every corner of her life? Would she ever have peace in this world of his? There was absolutely no way she was going to subject herself to this kind of uncertainty. She shuddered when she remembered she was willing to leave everything behind to be with him.

She'd waited for him for so long, not knowing he'd actually find her – because that's what had happened: he found her. But now that they were finally together, would she have been left waiting – waiting for him to call, for him to come home, for him to sort out his drama? Would she have spent the rest of her life far away from those who loved her to simply be alone, waiting?

No. She decided finally. This was not her life; she merely played a role in the biggest ruse in history. Her life – her real life – back home was beautiful and full and drama-free. No one tricked her and no one lied to her.

Shelby took a deep breath. She refused to cry. She'd leave on that flight home and wouldn't come back. She'd go back to living without Garridan Luca.

Garridan stretched as he opened his eyes. His back ached from the awkward position he was lying in. He sat up and looked around trying to remember why he'd fallen asleep with his shoes on. The room was dark, so he turned on the bedside lamp. The events of the day were slowly coming back to him.

He checked the time on his watch and was shocked to realise it was morning. The sleepless night he'd spent with Shelby combined with a draining interview, had exhausted him to a point where he could barely keep his eyes open when he left the radio station, so he returned to the hotel to rest for a bit. Had he been asleep all that time? Surely someone would've tried to wake him.

Panic seized him. He checked his watch again. Six forty-eight. "Shit! Shelby!" he cried. He searched his pockets for his phone. "What the hell?" he said when he realised the battery was dead. He needed to get to the airport.

Garridan fled the room and ran down the long corridor towards the elevators, pressing the buttons impatiently. Thankfully, it was still early, so the elevator arrived quickly and when he reached the basement garage where his car was parked, he startled a patrolling security guard by running across the lot to his car.

He immediately put his phone on charge and sped towards the airport, ignoring speed limits and skipping traffic lights where he could. He didn't care about being a responsible, law-abiding citizen. All he cared about was getting to the airport before Shelby boarded the flight. The departure time was at eight and although it was a short drive to the airport from the hotel, he feared he'd be too late. All he could do now was hope there'd be some kind of delay.

When he arrived at the airport, he parked his car haphazardly over a few parking bays, again not caring about the law. He ran as fast as he could and checked the information board for her flight. He found the correct boarding gate and approached the attendant there.

"Excuse me. Have the passengers for the flight to Johannesburg boarded yet?"

"Yes, sir. As per regulations," she indicated to the remaining people in the queue.

"Can you tell me if Shelby Wilson is on the plane already?" he asked as he cracked his knuckles.

"We're not allowed to divulge passenger information. Sorry." She didn't look sorry.

"Ple–"

"Garridan?" someone called, interrupting him.

Garridan looked around trying to locate the familiar voice between the sea of faces around him.

"Over here!"

Garridan smiled and walked towards Rodrigo.

"Hey, man. You're kinda late." Rodrigo said sympathetically as they shook hands.

"I was hoping there'd be a delay."

Rodrigo shook his head. "Sucks."

"Did she say anything?"

"Nah, she just cried," Rodrigo said sadly. "A lot."

Garridan's heart sank into the pit of his stomach. "Is she coming back?" he asked, still hopeful.

"I don't think so."

Rodrigo shook his head again and patted Garridan on the shoulder, a silent but friendly gesture of support – or condolence – Garridan wasn't sure. He nodded once in thanks.

They walked to the window and waited for the plane to take off. Rodrigo left immediately after but Garridan stayed and watched until the plane was just a speck in the sky.

He dropped heavily into one of the chairs at the window staring at the place where just a few minutes before, the plane that carried his love away from him stood. How could he have messed up so badly? He pictured Shelby's face and recalled their last night together. He remembered her playfulness just the morning before. Was she really not coming back?

His phone dinged, drawing his attention. He had so many messages. Some were from Marc and Quincy the previous night reminding him of their flight and arrangements for getting his car back to L.A. The others were from Shelby. The one that just came in was from Quincy: *Where the hell are you? We have a flight today.* Garridan quickly replied that he was on his way. Then he gave all his attention to Shelby's messages from the night before:

21:25 *Are you still coming?*

21:48 *If you're still busy, I'll understand but just let me know*

22:14 *Garridan, I'm freaking out. Please let me know if you're okay. I really hope you're okay*

Garridan opened a picture she'd sent.

22:53 *I hope she was worth it. Goodbye*

He looked at the picture. It was a screenshot of a social media post. Kimber had posted a picture of herself dancing at a party and Garridan frowned as he studied it. He remembered that night. It was from an event in L.A. The night he broke up with her. What did Shelby mean by it?

Enlarging the picture, his frown deepened as he saw the time the screenshot was taken displayed at the top; it was ten twenty-nine. The time on Kimber's post showed that she'd posted it fifty-three minutes before that. Garridan also noticed with surprise that she'd tagged him. His stomach roiled when he realised Shelby's assumption.

His despair was quickly replaced by anger. The depth of Kimber's deceit was unreal – posting something that was taken months before and making it seem recent, and tagging him as though he was with her. Was she deliberately trying to sabotage his relationship with Shelby? He knew she was unstable but this was taking it to a new level.

He stormed out of the airport. He should've dealt with Kimber when he saw her at the club. No, he should've dealt with her long before that, instead of hoping she'd simply vanish from his life after he called things off between them. He should've but he didn't and it cost him the love of his life.

On the way back to the hotel, Garridan's conscience nagged at him. As much as he despised what Kimber had done, he couldn't place all the blame on her. How could she have known he wasn't with Shelby and that her post would create so much animosity? It was just a cruel coincidence. He was part of the reason this mess had happened. He allowed himself to get carried away – interviews, meetings, the long trip to the cabin, clubbing. On a normal day, his life was full and stressful enough but with his need to spend as much time with Shelby before she left the country, instead of finding balance, he extended himself to the point of exhaustion. It was bound to catch up with him eventually.

His thoughts shifted to Shelby and a hollow sensation settled in his gut. He recalled Rodrigo's description of her – she cried a lot – and he tried to imagine her crying. It was such a foreign thought that even his imagination couldn't conjure such a vision.

Garridan considered the situation from Shelby's perspective and realised that, to her, he did exactly what her children's father did. Even though it wasn't what had really happened, it was what the twisted course of events led her to believe. It was her reality. Garridan laughed humourlessly at the incredulity of it all – just as the universe worked to bring them together, it strove to drive them apart. Like a sick, sadistic joke.

Guilt and sorrow instantly overcame him. He promised to protect Shelby but he hurt her instead. God, what has he done? A rogue tear rolled down his cheek. Whatever it took, he was going to fix this.

<h1 style="text-align:center">SHELBY</h1>

An overwhelming sense of relief washed over Shelby when she saw her sons' faces as she arrived home from the airport. She'd missed them terribly, and enjoyed catching up with them and basking in their affection.

Their family had arranged a small party welcoming her and Harlow home, and had gathered at Shelby's parents' house. She was glad to be back in the country and was grateful for the love she felt when she walked through the door and into her parents' arms. They plied her with kisses and complimented her healthy glow. She appreciated her family for wanting to spend time with her, but when their conversation turned to Garridan and her return to the U.S. to be with him, she wanted nothing more than to go to her own home and escape the embarrassing lies she fed them.

"Garridan and I aren't together anymore. I have so many projects lined up, I can't possibly think of anything else right now."

Harlow shot her a look of disapproval from across the room and Shelby shrugged apologetically.

"What are you doing?" Harlow asked later when they had some time alone.

"I can't tell them. Garridan doesn't need this kind of negative publicity," Shelby whispered.

"But you know they won't say anything."

"I know," Shelby sighed.

"What's *really* going on, Shel?"

Shelby dropped her head and pinched her eyes closed before she replied. "I don't want them to know," she said, looking pleadingly at Harlow. "I'm embarrassed – at my age, going through the same thing I experienced when I was in my twenties. All I want to do is curl up on my bed and think about what happened in Miami. Now that I'm far away from Garridan and everything that ruined what could have been the most amazing time of my life, I just want to process it all and put it behind me."

But leaving Garridan behind wasn't easy. He tried to contact her, but she deleted his messages without reading them. Nothing he could say would change the fact that he'd already proven who he wanted to be with. And although she longed for him, she had to move on. When her resistance started fading and the lure of his messages became too strong, she broke all contact and avoided anything that would remind her of him. It was the only way she'd get over him.

The months following her return were a blur. She smiled when she had to, interacted with others when she needed to, and did everything that was required of her. But she felt nothing. She was numb, functioning solely on autopilot.

Sleep eluded her as her mind kept wandering to Garridan. She wondered what he was doing, and if he was okay. Sometimes, people would raise concern about her weary appearance and she'd lie, saying she was hard at work with her writing. She acted excited about the prospects and pretended to be fine. If only they knew she was dying inside. She was forever altered and she'd never be the same woman she was before she met Garridan.

Spring had always been Shelby's favourite season. It brought new life and a feeling of happiness and hope. So when spring arrived, she thought things would be better. But nothing could have prepared her for the despair she'd face when Daniel moved out of their house and in with his brothers to be closer to his new internship, and Harlow's new adventure in Miami was about to start. She was immensely happy for them and proud of their achievements, but it felt as though she was losing everyone she loved and needed.

There were times she regretted going to Miami, and she was disappointed in herself for falling for Garridan so quickly. But there were also moments when she thought about their time together and considered herself lucky for having experienced a once-in-a-lifetime love.

By December, she'd grown accustomed to her new life. The sadness still followed her and she'd often catch herself wishing for Garridan like she did before. But time really did heal. She eventually accepted the past and slowly learnt to be happy again. And although she made plans and looked forward to the future, she promised herself to never, ever love another man again.

GARRIDAN

"And that's a wrap!" the director announced through the megaphone.

The cast and crew cheered. Filming was a great success.

Garridan exhaled with relief. He clapped, not in applause, but in an attempt to warm his hands. He was dressed warmly and wore gloves but the cold was creeping into his bones. He was tired, he was freezing, and he was eager to go home. Washington was good but he couldn't stand winter there. He needed sunny, warm Los Angeles. Thankfully, he'd be flying out the next day.

When he arrived at the hotel, he decided to take a hot, relaxing bath instead of having a quick shower. He needed the water to soak into him and soothe his worn body. He opened the taps and held a bottle over the stream as he poured a thick blue liquid into the tub.

In the bedroom, he looked for something warm to sleep in and started packing his suitcase for his trip home. His phone dinged with a message from Marc: *Two weeks' break. Filming in Atlanta starts in March. Lots to plan for.* Garridan smiled and replied with a quick thank you. It was a week before Christmas and he was so busy with his latest movie that he hadn't yet bought any gifts. Knowing he had some time off made him very happy.

When he returned to the bathroom, he lowered himself slowly between the bubbles. He'd always loved bubble baths. Where showers were invigorating, bubble baths were calming. He remembered how his mother used to pamper him – her only child – with them when he was just a little boy, and how special it made him feel.

A more recent memory also came to mind; one in which he felt just as special, but loved in a different way. It'd been five long and lonely months since he last saw her, last spoke to her. But her face and voice were emblazoned in his memory for eternity and for a brief, spellbinding second, it felt as though he could reach out and touch her. But the feeling vanished just as quickly. He sighed and wondered if he'd ever be able to take another bath without thinking about Shelby.

Leaning back against the tub, he closed his eyes and allowed the bubbles to work their magic.

SHELBY

The closing credits rolled on the screen before her. Everyone else had left as soon as the movie ended, but Shelby waited. The last time she saw his face or heard his voice was five painful months ago, so coming to the cinema to watch a movie that was produced long before they'd even met was a shock to her system. She sat glued to her seat, waiting for his name to scroll across the screen. And she stayed there even after it did.

"Ma'am?" a timid voice interrupted her thoughts.

A woman stood in the aisle next to her. She carried a broom and large plastic bag.

"Sorry," Shelby said softly.

She walked slowly through the cinema doors and into the bright, busy mall. The sights and sounds overwhelmed her senses that were already heightened as a result of seeing Garridan again. She wished Harlow was there. She really wanted to share her thoughts and hear her cousin's opinion about the movie, but it'd been two months since Harlow left for a job at an events management company in Miami, so she had no one to speak to. Even in the frenzy of the festive season, Johannesburg was a lonely place without her near.

She checked her watch and decided to grab an early supper before doing some last-minute Christmas shopping. She was hosting Christmas lunch this year and was determined to make it as special as possible. And with

Harlow and Rodrigo visiting between Christmas and New Year's Day, she had to make sure her usually sparse cupboards and fridge were stocked.

The restaurant hostess greeted her warmly when she arrived. "Table for one?" she asked.

"Yes, please."

They walked to a table towards the back.

"A waiter will be with you shortly," the hostess said, pulling the chair out slightly.

"Thank you," Shelby said with a smile and when the waiter arrived, she placed her order.

While she waited, she thought about the movie again. She thought about how Garridan was hers for a brief moment in time – she held his hand and kissed his lips and loved him. It was such a significant time in her life and it changed her completely but in the greater scheme of things, it was nothing. Insignificant. Just a drop of water in a vast ocean, not even causing a ripple.

When her food arrived, she sighed deeply and wondered what the point of it all was – them finding and loving each other against all odds, the big announcements. What was the point of going through all that only to lose it?

"What was the point?" she asked herself before digging in.

GARRIDAN

The flight home was uneventful but Garridan couldn't help smiling when he spotted Marc in the waiting area of the airport. They greeted each other with a brotherly hug.

"Welcome home," Marc said, clapping Garridan's back.

"Thank you," said Garridan with a sigh. "It's good to be home."

"Where to?" Marc asked when they reached his SUV.

"Home, please."

En route from the airport, Marc caught Garridan up on everything they'd been busy with while he was in Spokane. As his agent, Marc had been working hard lining up potential roles which were suitable for Garridan. Garridan didn't mind what the role was as long as he did what he loved and earned money doing it, but Marc felt he needed to get into bigger productions more frequently in order to stay relevant. Although Garridan understood the logic, Marc's choice of words made him feel more like a commodity than a person.

"I'd like us to meet tomorrow once you're settled to go over the roles," Marc said.

"I thought we have a two-week break."

"You do. But this is the last thing we need to speak about before you relax and put on some holiday weight," Marc chuckled and patted Garridan's belly. "Oh, and

Quincy wanted me to remind you that you still haven't responded to Rodrigo's invitation."

Garridan was hoping to avoid this conversation. He didn't know what to do. He and Rodrigo had stayed in touch after Shelby and Harlow left the country. They also met up a few times when Garridan travelled to Miami. And now that Harlow was living with him and their relationship was serious, they'd be flying to South Africa after Christmas to spend time with Harlow's family. Rodrigo planned to propose to her there and he'd already arranged a surprise engagement party because he was certain she'd say yes. Naturally, because of their mutual friendship, Garridan was invited.

"Hello?" Marc said as if Garridan had forgotten he was there.

Garridan sighed heavily. "I don't know what to do."

"Why not?"

"Shelby is Harlow's family; they're as close as sisters. It's a guarantee she'll be there. And if I go to South Africa, it wouldn't be for just a day, I'll have to stay for at least a week. I don't know what I'll do being that close to her for an entire week but not being able to touch her."

Marc nodded. "And what about Kimber?"

"What about her?" Garridan glared at him.

Marc briefly left the steering wheel and held his hands up in defence. "I'm just saying that Quincy's had his hands full with the amount of fires he's had to put out."

Garridan shot him a look that ended the discussion.

Marc simply shrugged and dropped it.

SHELBY

After dropping the shopping bags in the entrance hall, Shelby closed the door behind her and activated the alarm. She didn't plan on going anywhere else after the day she'd had.

She gathered the bags and lugged them to the kitchen. Pulling a list from a drawer, she reviewed her inventory, ticking off what she had and making a new list of what she still needed. With less than a week to go, she was growing increasingly excited about Christmas lunch. It'd been a while since anyone's been to her house. Her boys were out living and building their own lives, and she was the one who always visited everyone else. Everything was planned meticulously and the only thing left now was the cooking. Shelby didn't particularly enjoy cooking but she had help, so that added to the excitement she was feeling.

Once the groceries were packed away, she went into the living room to rest. Sitting on her favourite couch, she clicked through the TV channels while eating a microwave dinner. Unable to find something worthwhile to watch, she left the TV on some brainless celebrity news channel. She wasn't in the mood to think and while she absently watched, she scrolled through her phone.

After her experience with Garridan, he tried to contact her several times and left messages wherever he could, but she blocked him on every platform that gave him access to her. She also avoided social media and anything that might bring her news about him and Kimber. But as time passed, she learnt to accept the situation for what it was, and she was able to watch TV again and return to social media.

"....with actor Garridan Luca."

Shelby's head whipped as the words from the TV drew her attention.

"Luca's spy thriller was a major hit at the box office this week. Let's hear what he had to say," said the TV show's host.

The picture switched from the host and suddenly, Garridan's face filled the screen. Shelby's heart fluttered. She turned the volume up. It was a pre-recorded interview about the movie she'd watched that afternoon.

"The action scenes were the epitome of dangerous and the stunts were hard to pull off. But it was fun and worth all the bruises," Garridan said as he tipped his head and winked into the camera.

Shelby's stomach did a little flip.

"And how do you feel about becoming a father?" the reporter asked.

Shelby sat on the edge of the couch waiting for his answer.

"I–I–It's something I'll get used to once the baby is here," he stammered over the words.

"Have you and Kimber set a wedding date yet?"

The question knocked the wind out of Shelby.

"No comment," Garridan said with a frown and walked away.

The reporter turned back to the camera and said, "Let's not ruin the surprise."

Shelby lowered the volume and chewed her nails. Was he really going to marry Kimber? Why was he being so evasive? What would he have done if she did as they'd originally planned and stayed with him?

GARRIDAN

Garridan waved as Marc drove off. He rummaged through his bag for the front door key and was just about to unlock the door when he heard a car trekking up his driveway. Turning to see who it was, he tossed his head back and groaned irritably as Kimber scrambled out of her ostentatious SUV. Garridan's happy mood quickly fizzled and he rushed to get into his house.

"Good morning, honey," she greeted him cheerfully. "Welcome home," she added as she sashayed through the door behind him.

Not bothering with formalities, Garridan flung his keys onto the table and asked, "Why are you here, Kimber?"

"Can't a girl welcome home the father of her child?" she asked with a pout and held her hand to her chest.

Garridan snorted at her forced hurt expression and turned his back on her. "You don't know it's mine, remember?"

"I *do* know," she replied defensively.

"No, you don't. We agreed to a DNA test once the baby is here. So, in case you didn't hear me before, why are you here?" he asked again.

"I missed you and I just wanted to see you," Kimber whined.

"We spoke about this. You can't just show up here. We

have nothing to say to each other. You ruined every chance of a friendship after everything you've done."

"But what did I do?"

Garridan cringed at her obvious and poor attempt at sounding innocent.

"All the news about us that you keep leaking to the tabloids as a *reliable source*? Does that ring a bell?" he asked.

"I don't know what you're talking about!" she yelled.

"You can play dumb all you want, Kimber. But I'm on to you and if you don't stop spreading these rumours, I'll have no choice but to get my lawyers involved," he said, turning to glare at her.

Kimber swept her hair behind her ear and pushed her shoulders back. "If you *try* to humiliate me, Garridan, I'll ruin you. I promise. And you'll never see your child."

"Get out!" he shouted, walking over to her and nudging her towards the door. "I don't want you anywhere near me!"

Garridan hated speaking to her like that. He believed women should be respected and treated kindly. But Kimber had a way of bringing out the worst in him.

She stuck out her bottom lip. "Fine. I'll go!" she cried, turning on her heels and slamming the door as she left his house.

Garridan rubbed a hand across his face. He'd been looking forward to coming home. It was all he wanted for the last few weeks. He was miserable without Shelby and being home was his only solace. Now, even his sanctuary had been tainted by Kimber's constant and annoying presence. He couldn't believe this was his life. He couldn't believe that in about two months' time, he'd find out whether or not he'd be stuck with her for the rest of his life. He groaned again and flopped down onto the couch.

He thought about the brief discussion he and Shelby had about her not wanting any more children and he recalled that they never did finish their discussion, even after she finally agreed to stay with him. At the time, he didn't even know if he wanted children and now it was something he was forced to face whether he wanted to or not. But there were two things that were preventing him from pouring himself into it just yet: the possibility that the baby isn't his, and the fact that Kimber is its mother.

He recalled Kimber's behaviour a few minutes before. Her obnoxious, catty ways and the fact that she was attention-seeking are what made her so unattractive. Garridan couldn't help but compare her to Shelby. It was something he did often. They were worlds apart. Shelby's understated beauty, her charm and her intelligence were so alluring, but what made him tick was the many different ways in which she loved him. The adoration in her eyes when she looked at him always, *always* drove him to a point where he wanted to lose himself in her. Nothing about Kimber told him anything about her supposed feelings for him. She was just as superficial and fake on the inside as she was on the outside, whereas Shelby was an abyss of mystery, class and poise. He would've loved to raise a child with her.

A dull ache in Garridan's chest had been there since the day she left. In a way, he didn't want it to ever go away. It was a reminder of what was. He lost something amazing when he lost her and if a handful of photos and heartache were the only remnants of what they had, he'd gladly keep them.

He pulled his phone from his pocket and looked at the photos he and Shelby took at the beach on their first date. He looked at them all the time but he never got tired of them. He'll treasure the memory of that day forever.

Garridan jerked when his phone rang. He'd fallen asleep with Shelby on his mind and thought it was her calling, but it was Marc confirming a time for their meeting the next day. Quincy and Megan would join them.

After the call, he dragged himself to his bedroom, taking along his bags. He'd been home for nearly four hours but he hadn't gotten further than the living room. He unpacked his bags and changed into some gym clothes. He was a member of the local health club, but he converted one of the unused rooms in his house to a workout area for the days he didn't feel like being recognised and interrupted. He appreciated his supporters without a doubt but sometimes he just wanted to be himself, not someone famous. Again, his mind wandered to Shelby who didn't let on that she knew who he was until he asked her. She even let him introduce himself. He laughed at the memory of it.

Working out was something he both enjoyed and needed. But the need for it had nothing to do with aesthetics or acting or even fitness. It was the release he looked for when he needed to regain control of his life. While filming, the character he played superseded him as a person and the director dictated how, where and when he should do things. After months of filming, a good workout session was an amazing way for him to get out of character and back to himself. And apart from his work, the fact that Kimber had such tight control of his future because of the baby she was carrying, Garridan needed the extra boost and simultaneous release that only a good workout session could provide.

He spent a long time in the gym and did a variety of routines to help him get back the balance he so desperately needed. The best, though, was ramming his fists into the punching bag over and over until his arms felt heavy and fatigued. He wasn't an aggressive person but the mounting tension from every direction incited such rage inside him that he felt like bursting. As he hung breathlessly onto the bag in a state of complete exhaustion, he tried to remember a time when his life was serene. There was only one time, he thought, as he shoved himself from the bag. "She continues to undo me."

The following day, he met with his team. They gave him a rundown of the projects lined up and the tentative schedule planned for after New Year. They all had vacations to look forward to and would be back and ready to work by the second week of January.

Garridan listened to them intently, taking in all the information he needed to plan his personal life around. He then realised everyone he considered a close friend had plans for the holidays and none of it included him. They were all going away. His parents were the only family he had and they were already travelling in Europe, visiting friends. For the first time in his life, he would be alone for the holidays.

"Garridan?" Megan patted his hand from across the table. She looked at him expectantly.

"Sorry," he said, clearing his throat.

"Is there anything you need me to do before we leave?" She pointed between her and Marc who were flying to Italy the next morning.

Garridan considered the question and weighed his options. "Will you accept Rodrigo's invitation and book a flight to Johannesburg, please?" He avoided their stunned expressions. "And please check if there's room at the hotel the agency uses sometimes."

After the meeting, they wished each other well for the holidays and huddled together while Quincy said a prayer, asking for guidance and protection. As they went their separate ways, Garridan silently added to the prayer, asking for a way to accept and make peace with his situation.

The day before Christmas, Shelby buzzed around her house making sure everything was spotlessly clean and tidy for her lunch the next day.

The house was much bigger than the apartment she and the boys first lived in – the one she rented with their father before he abandoned them. She wanted better for her children, wanted to give them a good home in a good neighbourhood, so she struggled through distance learning courses while working fulltime at a dead end job. But eventually, she graduated and started her new career which allowed her to buy a wonderful home. One her sons could always call their own. As daunting as it was to take the leap and leave behind all the memories made in their old place, Shelby had always relied on her need to be a good mother to drive her. Parenthood was undoubtedly both the most fulfilling and the scariest role of her life. No one had prepared her for the amount of decisions and sacrifices she'd have to make for the sake of her children.

But she was glad for the change this one decision brought because it meant she could host her guests in comfort, and she could accommodate Harlow and Rodrigo who could choose from any of the bedrooms that were no longer in use.

As she wiped down the furniture, her thoughts shifted to Garridan. She wondered what kind of father he'd be. Would he be loving and hands-on, dealing with issues with open-mindedness? Or would he be strict and detached with an old school do-as-I-say attitude? She finally decided he'd be a kind, loving and attentive father who'd always want what's best for his children. Although the thought of him being with someone else still hurt, her insides felt warm and happy knowing he was going to become a father and that he'd also get to experience parenthood.

At around four o'clock, her sons came by to help with the moving of furniture. She was expecting quite a few guests and had to rearrange the dining room in a way that would be comfortable for everyone. The garden furniture also had to be moved to make way for the gazebo she got for the children. The rental chairs and tables for the kids would be delivered within the next hour.

They chatted excitedly as they worked and Shelby occasionally gave them refreshments. Although it was close to evening, the sun was still high and the weather was still hot, so with all the hard work, they needed hydration.

As she was washing up the afternoon's dishes, the front gate's intercom buzzed.

"Hey guys, I think the kids' chairs are here. Can someone check and open for the delivery van, please?" she hollered from the kitchen.

Shortly afterwards, she heard Daniel speaking and a muffled response came over the intercom. Shelby had just started polishing the silverware they'd be using the next day, when Daniel spoke again from the kitchen entrance.

"Mom," he said, trying to get her attention.

She held up a finger gesturing for him to wait while she counted out some dessert spoons.

"Mom," he repeated more urgently.

She stopped counting and looked up with a huff. But what she saw, took her breath away. In her kitchen, living, breathing and smiling as brightly as the sun outside, stood Garridan Luca.

Her jaw dropped and so did the spoons she was counting. They clattered loudly to the floor causing her to flinch.

"Hi, Shelby," he said.

A jolt coursed through her when he said her name. Shelby lost all her senses as she stood glued to one spot, speechless, staring at him. When she still didn't move, Garridan dropped his bags and walked slowly towards her as if she needed to be approached carefully.

From the corner of her eye, she watched Daniel leave the kitchen. It drew her out of her stupor and back to the moment. And without thinking, she closed the gap between her and Garridan, and launched herself into his arms.

Garridan chuckled as she slammed into is chest. His arms instantly wound around her body, locking her against him. His voice vibrated through her and into her soul. It was as if a part of her that was long lost had finally been returned. She finally felt whole. She didn't know, until that moment, just how much she'd missed him.

Shelby clung to Garridan like he was her lifeline. Hot tears soaked the front of his shirt but he didn't care. He caressed her hair and cooed into her ear, trying to console her. They stood like that for what seemed like forever when she finally released him and rubbed her hand down the front of his shirt, ironing it where their embrace had caused a crease. He chuckled again. She was so adorable.

"Hi," she finally said, smiling as she wiped her tears. "Wha–How?"

She struggled with the words but he knew what she wanted to ask. He picked the spoons up from the floor and handed it to her before settling into one of the barstools.

"Rodrigo invited me to the engagement party. The only flight Megan could get before the New Year, departed two days before. The hotel we made a reservation with, had to evacuate the floor my room was on after a ceiling collapsed. Everywhere else was full. Thankfully, before I left L.A., Rodrigo gave me this address. I didn't know it was your house until I saw Daniel. If I didn't come here, I would've been stranded." He rushed through his explanation, hoping it would relay why he appeared at her house so suddenly and unannounced.

Shelby put the spoons into the sink and leaned against the counter. "I'm glad you're here and safe and not stranded."

"Come here," he said, holding his arms out to her. He

missed her so damn much and holding her again revived his feelings for her. Reinforced it.

She stood between his legs. He folded his arms around her waist as she wrapped hers around his neck. Minutes ticked by. Their embrace was interrupted when her sons entered the kitchen. Shelby quickly backed out of Garridan's arms and introduced him to them. They joined him around the table in friendly conversation while she prepared a meal for them to enjoy.

After the boys left and it was just the two of them, Garridan could sense some uneasiness in Shelby now that the shock of seeing him so unexpectedly had worn off. They were in the living room, seated in silence on the couch. Images flickered across the screen of the muted TV, which Shelby stared at as though she was watching something interesting.

"You okay?" he asked.

She nodded. "I think I'm still a little overwhelmed. Sorry."

"You don't have to apologise. I shouldn't have just pitched up at your door without asking but I didn't know what else to do. I'll look for something else in the morning."

She frowned and shook her head. "You did the right thing. Don't even worry about it. I'm glad you're here."

"Thank you. I'm glad I'm here too." He scrubbed a hand across his stubble and yawned.

Shelby checked the time. "You must be tired," she said. "Let me show you where everything is, so you can get settled."

She grabbed one of his bags and he followed her as she showed him around the house. The bedrooms were upstairs and two of the three rooms he could choose from had en suite bathrooms. He looked into each of them. They were all beautifully and comfortably furnished.

"Which one is yours?" he asked.

She showed him.

"I'll take this one if it's okay," he asked, pointing to the one across the passage from hers.

"That's fine," she nodded.

Shelby changed the bedding, and showed him where the clean towels and other necessities were. While he unpacked, he heard her shuffling around in the adjoining bathroom and the sound of water running soon followed. When she returned to the room, she told him to check on the water in a few minutes' time, and left.

Later, when Garridan entered the bathroom, his heart swelled when he saw that she'd prepared a bubble bath for him. He closed the door, got undressed and sank into the cloud of bubbles. The water was perfect. Shelby was perfect. Her sons were perfect. He was content and he was happy.

He closed his eyes and relaxed in the soothing water.

* * *

The bed dipped under Garridan's weight but Shelby barely stirred. He slipped under the covers next to her. She was so warm. He pulled her into his side, fluffed the pillows and settled onto them with her in his arms.

She mumbled his name and wrapped her arm around

his waist, snuggling into the space that was made just for her.

He breathed deeply, finally able to relax, and drifted off into a deep, peaceful sleep.

When Shelby woke up on Christmas morning, Garridan was wrapped around her from behind. She pursed her lips to suppress a smile. A giddy feeling bubbled inside her. She still couldn't believe he was really there. With her. In her home. In her bed. It was real, not just a fantasy that played out on a dream vacation like some kind of fairy tale.

She lay quietly and listened to his soft breathing. She felt the rise and fall of his chest. One of his arms stretched out from under her neck and the other draped loosely over her waist. Their legs were a tangled mess. She fitted into him perfectly.

She reached out to check the time on her phone but Garridan stirred and pulled her closer as if to say 'you're not going anywhere'. She relaxed into him. It was still early. The alarm she'd set hadn't even gone off yet, so she closed her eyes again and relished the moment. She took in every detail – his cheek resting against her head, his muscular chest against her back, his scent, the smoothness of his skin, the softness of his arm hairs beneath her fingertips, the top of his thighs against the bottom of hers, their tangled feet. Everything. All senses engaged to sear that moment into her mind forever. She wanted to remember it always. Because it wasn't going to happen again. It shouldn't have happened in the first place. Garridan was in a relationship, he was going to get married and he was going to become a father. He shouldn't be in her bed. What would it say about him if he did it again? And what would it say about her if she allowed it?

The shrill buzz of the alarm jerked Shelby from her sleep and she silenced it quickly so as not to wake Garridan. Thankfully, he wasn't wrapped around her anymore, so she lifted his hand from her thigh in a slow, soft motion and escaped to her bathroom.

She turned on the shower and headed to the basin to brush her teeth. Her mind was reeling with everything she had to do before her guests arrived. The large pot of food alone would consume about one and a half hours of her time. The tables had to be set and decorated, and she decided to set up a place on the patio for the kids to play. She'd have to take some of the boys' old toys out from storage.

Looking into the mirror, she studied her reflection. Her eyes were clear, her skin was glowing and she had a soft pink blush in her cheeks. Her lips were plump and red from just having brushed her teeth. Inside, her heartbeat was light and steady. Excitement coursed through her. The joy she felt was heady. She felt alive.

She didn't recognise the woman in the mirror. The one who stared back at her the past few months had bloodshot eyes surrounded by dark circles, sallow skin, and pursed lips. Inside, her heartbeat was heavy, her breaths were pained and she carried a perpetual knot in her stomach.

When did she transform? Was it because of Garridan?

She shook off the thought and stood under the hot,

rejuvenating water. No. She wasn't going down that road again. Maybe he *was* good for her and maybe she *did* need him in her life. It was wonderful to see him again and to hold him, and he obviously felt the same because he slipped into bed with her. But it was too late for love. He already belonged to someone else, so she can never act on her feelings. If he were to be in her life, it would never be romantic. She'd accept his friendship if that's all she was destined to have, but she'd have to control her emotions if she wanted it to work. She'd have to do what Garridan did when he was acting – divorce the character from her real self. She decided finally that that was what she'd do. It would only be for a few days while he was there and when he returned to L.A., she'd be free to love him from a distance. Once again, she'd be a star on a stage. Only this time, it would be a solo performance.

GARRIDAN

Garridan woke to the sound of a shower running. He stretched and allowed his eyes to adjust to the brightness of the room. It was a beautiful South African Christmas morning – sunny and warm.

He turned his attention to the bathroom door. Shelby mentioned she'd be up early to finish preparations for Christmas lunch. Apparently, he'd be meeting most of her family.

"No pressure," he mumbled as he stared up at the ceiling.

His mind was running a thousand miles a minute. A marathon of thoughts buzzing around, pleading for his attention. But he wasn't ready to address them yet. Not now.

He groaned as he sat up on the bed. He wished he could rest a little while longer but since Shelby was up, he had to do the same. He was the only one with her, so he should help with the preparations wherever he could. He stared longingly at the closed bathroom door. There was nothing he wanted more than to join her in the shower. But he didn't know how she felt about him crawling into bed with her, so he abandoned the thought and went to his assigned room across the passage.

After his shower, Garridan stared at the clothes he'd packed away the night before. He didn't know what the dress code for lunch was but from what he saw, it looked like a formal affair. He grabbed a formal shirt and pants, and laid it on the bed for later.

As he was about to get dressed, a soft k nock o n the door interrupted him. He only had a towel around his waist but with no one other than them in the house, he answered, "Come on in."

The door swung open slowly and Shelby peeked into the room, her body hidden behind the door. "Are you decent?" she asked.

He looked down at the towel. "As decent as can be," he replied with a chuckle. "Come in."

She closed the door behind her. "Merry Christmas," she said with a smile.

He walked towards her with his arms outstretched. "Merry Christmas," he said and pulled her in for a hug which she returned awkwardly.

He went back to the closet and retrieved a brightly-coloured package from under his t-shirts. He held it behind his back as he returned to her. "Merry Christmas," he said again and handed the gift to her.

She gasped. "Garridan, you really shouldn't have," she said. "I–I didn't get you anything."

He chuckled. "You didn't know I was coming."

"Yeah, I didn't," she finally smiled. "Thank you. This is really sweet."

Garridan stared at her. She didn't even know what it was but she was already grateful.

"Open it," he said.

She sat on the edge of the bed and looked at him thoughtfully. Garridan watched her closely as she chewed on her lip. Something was different. Off. She looked scared. No, nervous. Did he make her nervous?

Her eyes eventually left his and she turned her attention to her gift. She opened it gently as if she didn't want to tear the wrapping, which she folded neatly and placed on the bed. She looked up at Garridan again when she saw the rectangular blue box. There was sadness in her eyes.

"I can't accept this," she said, shaking her head.

Garridan frowned. "What do you mean?"

"It's too much."

"But you haven't even opened it yet," he said incredulously.

She shook her head again. "I'm sorry, Garridan. Thank you, but I can't accept this," she repeated, holding the box out to him.

He took it gingerly, watching her again. Something was definitely wrong. She avoided his eyes and looked down at her hands, picking at her pretty Christmas-themed nail polish. Concerned, Garridan sat beside her. He put the box on the bed and took her hands in his, caressing them lovingly.

"What's wrong?" he asked.

"Nothing," she replied softly but wouldn't look at him.

"I can tell something's wrong. What is it?"

She peeked at him from under her lashes. "Garridan, I don't think we should sleep together anymore." She flinched as if her own words hurt her.

Garridan's heart flipped and his stomach twisted. "Why not?" he asked, dropping her hands as he stood and walked to the window furthest from her. He sensed her following him. He leaned heavily against the window sill, his back towards her. Was this really happening? He was losing her again. "Why don't you want to sleep with me?" he repeated.

He was tired of dancing around their feelings. Their love. It was obvious they had a lot to talk about. They both had a lot to say, but neither of them had the courage to say anything. He was tired, so tired of it! He wanted to speak and he wanted to speak to her! And he wanted to hear what she needed to say.

"It's not that I don't want to. We *can't*. It's not right," she said.

Her voice was even and when he looked over his shoulder at her, her expression betrayed nothing. Poker face, he thought.

"Why not?" he asked, facing her. "What's so wrong about us sleeping together? It's not like we're having sex!" He sounded like a wounded child but he didn't care. He just wanted to understand. Then a thought occurred to him. "There's someone else, isn't there?"

His knees nearly gave in when she nodded.

"Yes, Garridan, there is someone else." Her voice was stern and her nostrils flared slightly.

Was she angry?

"In fact, there are two!" she added.

This time, he nearly passed out. "What the hell are you talking about?" he asked, his tone matching hers.

Her hands flew to her hair, then up towards the ceiling before it fell gracelessly, slapping her thighs, as if she couldn't believe how clueless he was.

"I'm talking about Kimber and your baby!" she said, pointing to the corner.

Garridan's eyes followed her hand and he noticed the TV. He frowned. "What about them? This has nothing to do with them!"

Shelby's eyes widened. She looked stunned, disgusted even. "How can this"–she gestured between him and her–"not have anything to do with them? Did you forget you're getting married?" She glared at him and folded her arms across her chest.

Garridan's dumbstruck expression made Shelby wonder what exactly bewildered him; the fact that he was getting married or the fact that she knew.

He sat on the bed and buried his face in his hands, his elbows resting on his knees. "I can't believe this," he said, his words muffled by his hands.

"What can't you believe? Did you think I wouldn't find out?" she asked, voicing her thoughts. "Do you think that just because I live on another continent, I'd be oblivious?"

Garridan looked at her but was frozen in his bewildered state.

"I was a summer fling to you in Miami, Garridan," she continued. "One day, you introduced me to the world as your girlfriend and the next, you were with Kimber. It was humiliating. Do you want me to be your summer fling here too, so you can embarrass me in front of my family?"

She didn't give him a chance to answer. She wasn't going to be mesmerised by his charm this time. There was no going back now. The floodgates that had been sealed for five months have finally been opened. No more pretending. No more acting.

"You hurt me, Garridan! I had to come home and face my family and explain why I wasn't going back to you anymore. I had to *lie* to them, feed them some bullshit story just to hide my pain! Then I had to hide my pain every day since. It was killing me slowly and there was nothing I could do about it!" she sobbed and crawled onto the other side of the bed.

"Knowing you had your way with me, then ditched me to party with Kimber was the worst thing anyone's ever done to me! And people did pretty shitty things to me before. You made me question my worth as a person. I promised myself I wouldn't cry for you. I wanted to be strong. But when you didn't even bother seeing me off at the airport, it broke me! I was so torn. I bawled like a baby in front of Harlow and Rodrigo! Did you even care about my feelings, Garridan?"

She hiccoughed and wiped wildly at the tears that were now streaming down her cheeks as she tried to regain control of her emotions. She didn't mean to bare her soul, or to cry, but she was through hiding from him. She needed him to know exactly what he'd done to her. She took a deep, calming breath and focused on her heartbeat. How was it possible that he still invoked this level of emotion from her?

When she looked at Garridan, his expression was pained as if it was the first time he'd heard about this. It reignited her anger. He was such a good actor that he was putting on a performance at that moment to cover up his actions. She wasn't falling for it.

"Why are you looking at me like that? It's not as if you didn't know what you did to me. You were there when you did it!"

GARRIDAN

As hurt and angry as Garridan was, his priority was Shelby who sat on the bed hugging her legs to her chest, her chin on her knees. She looked absolutely miserable and it was entirely his fault. He walked to the other side of the bed and sat slowly beside her, afraid he'd anger her even more. He knew she didn't want or need his touch right then, but he wanted to help her.

"Baby–"

"Don't call me that!" she cut him off and sniffed back more tears.

"Sorry." He started again, "Shelby. Shel, I'm really sorry I got into bed with you last night. I haven't been sleeping well without you. And I just needed to be close to you again. I missed you. I miss you." She didn't respond, so he continued, "I can see how hurt you are by everything that's happened but I promise you, I *promise* you, it's not what you think."

This was harder than he thought. How could he have been so stupid? How could he have thought that her bad experience before she left Miami would have been forgotten? How could he think they could just pick up where they left off? She wasn't used to the craziness of his world – the world of fame where everyone did and said whatever they wanted without caring about the consequences. He had years and years of experience and was desensitised against the rumours, the insults, the hate, and even things that appeared to be great but were actually false. Did he really think she'd just eventually get over Kimber's post when his absence exacerbated the perception it cause? How could he have thought she'd forget about it with time, when he appeared to betray her just like her ex did?

"Shel, please?" he pleaded. "Listen to me. There's an explanation for everything. But now isn't the time to talk about it. You have guests coming over and I don't want your day to be ruined."

He's never imagined she could look so small, so fragile, so defeated. It hurt him to see her like that. And he hated himself for being the cause of it.

"Can we talk about it tonight after everyone's left?" he asked hopefully. "That is, if I can still stay here."

She shrugged and closed her eyes as if in prayer. When she opened them again, she nodded. "We can talk. And you can stay."

That was all. She stood and left the room. Left her gift. Left him.

Garridan was right. Although they needed to have a serious talk, there were more pressing things that required her attention. She was already running late, no thanks to her outburst.

Her body was still buzzing from all the emotions coursing through it. She had to work hard to compose herself as she walked out of Garridan's room. Her heart ached when she saw the look on his face. She didn't mean to lash out and she didn't mean to hurt him. She was just too confused about everything. They were perfect together; they clearly still loved each other. They were a chance in eight billion, literally. So why did everything work against them? Why did he want to rekindle what they had when he knew they couldn't be together?

After washing her face, she left her room, stopping across the passage at his door. She knocked and waited for his reply.

"Come in," his muffled voice wafted through the door.

She peered into the room. He was dressed in a t-shirt and shorts, and was tying his shoelaces.

"I came for your clothes. They need to be ironed." She pointed to his clothes on the bed, which she'd seen earlier but forgot to take with her when she left the room.

"Thank you," he said, handing the clothes to her. Then he smiled, asking, "So, what do you need me to help you with?"

They left the room together as if nothing had happened. Shelby ran down a list of things he could help with while she cooked and decorated the tables. She also had to collect the other food from the ladies who'd offered to help out.

Nearly an hour later, while she was stirring a massive pot on the stove, Garridan entered the kitchen holding some toys in his hands. He'd been unpacking things from storage for the kids to play with later. He held up his hands.

"Where am I?" he asked, looking at her with a raised eyebrow.

She frowned. "What do you mean?"

He held his hands out showing her the toys. "Where. Am. I?" he asked again pointedly.

Shelby walked over to him and laughed when she saw the Ultimate Combatants action figures he was holding. She covered her face with her hands as she laughed uncontrollably. She couldn't believe she'd have to answer that question.

"Shel, I'm serious. This isn't funny," he grumbled.

He couldn't possibly be offended that the toy of his character, Sergeant Jameson, wasn't in the boxes, could he?

She recovered from her fit of laughter. She was embarrassed to tell him but she did anyway, "It's in my room."

Garridan puffed his chest, looking utterly satisfied with her answer and with himself. "Okay," he said, giving her a dashing smile before strutting off to finish his task.

Shelby could only shake her head in disbelief. Which other woman on the planet was telling her celebrity crush slash semi-boyfriend slash temporary housemate that a toy in his likeness was in her bedroom? No one, she thought. No other woman.

It was nearly time for her guests to arrive. Shelby and Garridan had finished setting up well ahead of her schedule, which gave them enough time to do themselves up. Shelby laughed at the thought. Garridan didn't need much doing up; he practically woke up already perfect. She decided to wear a pretty but comfortable chiffon dress and because she'd be doing a lot of walking, she opted for ballet flats instead of heels.

She was downstairs checking on dessert in the fridge when Garridan joined her. She turned when she heard his footsteps and nearly dropped the bowl she was carrying. His hair was gelled back which caused his blue eyes to appear more striking and his stubble more appealing. The shirt and pants that looked so plain when she ironed them earlier, now graced his perfect, muscular frame. Combined with his formal shoes, he looked like he was about to step onto a runway instead of have lunch with her family.

"Whoa!" she exclaimed as she gripped the bowl.

He rushed to help and the manly fragrance of his cologne invaded her nostrils.

"Sorry," he said. "Did I startle you?"

"No, it's my fault. I got distracted," she replied. "You look h–handsome," she stammered, feeling her face flush.

His eyes raked over her from head to toe and this time, her entire body blushed. She put the bowl into the fridge before she really dropped it.

"Thank you. And you look beautiful, Shel," he said in a deep, alluring voice. His gaze pierced hers.

"Thank you," she whispered, unable to tear her eyes from his.

The pull between them was undeniable. Shelby loved the adoration and the desire she saw in his gaze, and she wasn't sure how much longer she'd be able to resist him. Although she told him they shouldn't sleep in the same bed, it was hard having him so close to her and not being able to act on her emotions. Sometimes she yearned for just a simple touch, but she knew better. She wouldn't lead him on.

The intercom buzzed, jerking her from her dazzled state. The first of her guests had arrived.

"Ready?" he asked softly.

"Yes. Come with me?" she asked.

He nodded and they walked to the front gate to welcome her guests.

As they walked along the footpath, Garridan glanced at Shelby from the corner of his eye. She looked so pretty. Her dress was so appealing on her. The soft colour matched the blush of her cheeks, and the light fabric fluttered in the gentle breeze. He loved the way she did her hair. It was longer than he remembered but it was soft and glossy and resembled liquid ink. With the pretty shoes she wore, she looked like royalty.

She introduced him to the different family members as they arrived and at some point, when Shelby had her hands full with the guests already there, Garridan took it upon himself to welcome those who arrived afterwards. He enjoyed it very much.

Once everyone was settled, Shelby cleared her throat to welcome them formally.

"Hi, everyone. Merry Christmas," she said, smiling warmly as they returned her greeting. "Thank you for coming over today to celebrate this special day. I'm honoured to be able to spend it with you." Her eyes settled briefly on Garridan. "Thank you to everyone who prepared the delicious meals because it would *not* have been so great to eat anything I prepared." Her boys nodded and everyone laughed. "I'm really blessed to have you in my life. I love you all dearly."

After an applause and hugs, Shelby's mother blessed the meal and her father made a sweet little speech. It was all so genuine and unrehearsed, and Garridan now understood why Shelby was such an amazing person. She was deeply loved and smothered with affection. Where love was concerned, she lacked nothing.

Her family was beautiful. Apart from their welcoming friendliness, they were an eclectic mix of colours, shapes, sizes, names and accents. They also switched between two languages as they spoke to each other, though he could tell that most of them were predominantly English-speaking. Garridan had never seen a family as diverse as this one. He was fascinated and enjoyed watching them interact with each other and appreciated that they included him as if he'd been part of their family since birth – just another member of their large family.

The food was amazing! Garridan ate dishes he'd never tasted before. The names were the same – biryani, chicken curry, roast lamb – but the flavours were out of this world. He ate a little bit of everything and was sure he'd gain the holiday weight Marc had teased him about.

Dessert was no different. There were so many to choose from that he didn't know where to start. He watched as Shelby dished something that looked like a dark sponge cake and poured hot custard over it. It was strange but he wanted the whole experience, so he did the same. He closed his eyes as the blend of flavours and textures melted on his tongue.

"It's malva pudding," Shelby's aunt said from across the table and she explained how it was made.

"It's delicious," he said sincerely.

Shelby's mother handed him a bowl of something cold.

"Daniel made this," she said, glancing proudly at her grandson who looked embarrassed.

Shelby giggled and leaned towards Garridan. "We'll go to the gym before you leave."

"I can't believe you've eaten nearly as much as me," he said, laughing before he winked at Daniel and dug in.

His dessert was a winner: cold, a balance of sweet and rich, tangy fruit and a hint of chocolate. When he was done, he gave Daniel a thumbs up and the young man smiled back in appreciation.

After lunch, everyone sat back and enjoyed each other's company. Harlow's sister was on photo duty, so she walked around with a camera dangling from her neck, taking candid shots. No posing, no preparation. Everyone was captured in the moment.

Occasionally, various groups of women would go to the kitchen to wash up the dishes that had accumulated during the gathering. The ever-considerate Shelby would protest, but it was obvious they did it because they cared for her. Garridan's heart swelled to know she was so well-loved.

It was fun and so heartwarming watching Garridan with her crazy family. She knew it would be that way. They welcomed everyone as if they'd always belonged. That Garridan was a huge Hollywood star didn't take away the fact that he was a person first, and that's what mattered most to them.

But what stole Shelby's heart was seeing him with her sons. She'd never seen her boys so engaged with someone who wasn't their age. They usually disappeared to their own little corners of the house to do whatever it was they enjoyed; but not today. Today, Garridan had all their attention. They were so engrossed and so animated, Shelby wondered if he was dazzling them with his charm like he did her.

Cindy was taking photos, so Shelby called her closer. "Please take a photo of them?" she asked, pointing at her guys.

"Already did," she winked and showed Shelby a beautiful shot that melted her heart. "I'll have it blown up and framed. It'll be my gift to you," she said and kissed Shelby on the cheek before she continued capturing more precious moments.

After a while, the smaller kids got restless. They'd been waiting all day for their gifts. Although they received gifts at their own homes that morning, they were excited because Santa was coming. The kids couldn't contain their elation when he shouted, "Ho, ho, ho!" from the garden and walked towards the sliding doors. The adults enjoyed their excitement and laughed at Santa's reaction when the kids charged and nearly knocked him down with the force.

The Christmas tree was set up just inside the patio door, with a special chair on the one side just for Santa. The kids finally settled down when he took his seat and emptied his bag of gifts under the tree.

Shelby glanced at Garridan who was sitting across the room from her. A broad smile graced his face as he sat comfortably between her twins, Seth and Oliver. And as Santa started picking up gifts, Garridan sat forward in his seat with his elbows perched on his knees. He looked so thoughtful, Shelby wondered what he was thinking in that moment. One by one the kids were called until they all received their gift and left to play together in the area Garridan had set up.

Then it was the adults' turn.

When Shelby planned the lunch, the family agreed to play Secret Santa to ensure everyone received a gift. Now the adults seemed just as excited as the kids were when Santa emptied his second bag and started calling out names. The pile of gifts got smaller and smaller as Santa handed them out. When there were only a few left, he picked up one that made Shelby's heart leap.

"Garridan!" he called.

Shelby watched as a look of surprise momentarily crossed Garridan's features, but he recovered quickly and smiled, his acting skills coming into play.

Everyone watched as he collected his gift with thanks.

Shelby's heart drummed so hard she could hear it. And when Garridan's gaze locked with hers as he returned to his seat, she knew that whatever they'd been fighting was over.

GARRIDAN

It was nearing evening and only a few relatives lingered. As lovely as the day was, Garridan couldn't wait for everyone to leave. It wasn't that he didn't enjoy himself; in fact, today could possibly have been one of his favourite days. But he was eager to be alone with Shelby and he couldn't wait any longer. The way she looked, the amazing atmosphere, and her little glances throughout the day made him crave alone time with her.

They were standing at the gate, waving as another car drove off. His hand rested on her lower back and she leaned into him. When she turned towards the house, he wrapped his arms around her waist, stopping her. She looked up at him with a raised eyebrow.

He chuckled. "Am I still banned from your bed?"

"Yes, Garridan," she mumbled.

"You're not banned from mine," he said, waggling his eyebrows.

She laughed but didn't say anything.

"Are we going to talk tonight?" he asked, studying her face.

She nodded. "I'd like to if you're up for it."

He let go of her waist and held her hand as they walked slowly back to the house. "I'm up for anything that will fix things between us."

They strolled in silence. Her hand was warm in his and Garridan relished how she fit him perfectly. It was as if she was created just for him. He pulled her into his side and draped his arm around her neck. She didn't protest; she simply wrapped her arm around his waist.

As they entered the house, Seth told Shelby they'd already packed up the things that were set up in the garden and patio, and that the rest of the guests were ready to leave.

"You don't have to walk back to the gate, Mom. We'll see them out," he said, gesturing to his brothers.

Shelby thanked him and hugged each of her sons affectionately. She thanked them for helping and asked them to drive safely. It was heartwarming watching her with them and, again, Garridan thought about how he would've loved to raise a child with her. He couldn't picture Kimber like that.

While Shelby greeted her mother and the last of her guests, Garridan said goodnight to her sons.

"Thank you. It was a really great day," he said, shaking their hands.

As they waited to see the lasts guests off, they spoke to Garridan and laughed at the witty jokes Oliver told. They were easy-going and friendly, and not what he'd expected at all. He expected them to give him a hard time for what he did to their mom, but when he remembered she lied to them to hide her humiliation, a knot formed in his stomach. That was another thing he'd have to fix.

On her way out, Shelby's mother took his hand in hers and looked up at him with a smile. "You bring out the best in my daughter," she said and placed a motherly kiss on his cheek.

Pride swelled in his heart. "And she brings out the best in me," he said, closing his hand around hers. "Thank you for today."

"It was our pleasure," she replied, beaming as she walked off with her grandsons.

Garridan locked and armed the house, and they headed upstairs. Shelby looked tired but she chatted excitedly about their day.

"I'm so happy it went well," she said, grinning. "What did you think?"

"It was lovely. And your family is really amazing, especially your sons."

"Thank you, Garridan. And thank you for helping me today."

"It was nothing. I enjoyed it."

They walked down the passage and stopped in the space that separated their rooms.

"I'm just going to freshen up and change, then we can talk. Is that okay?" she asked.

"Sounds good. I'll see you in a bit?"

She entered her room and closed the door.

In his room, Garridan sat on the bed thinking about the day. Although he had a great time, Shelby's words that morning played on his mind, '...it broke me'. And the sad look in her eyes haunted him. He had the entire day to think about what he was going to tell her tonight. It seemed so simple: explain what really happened, answer all her questions, tell her how he feels. Simple. But the more time he spent with her and the more he saw her in her own space, the deeper he fell and the more complicated the words got in his head. He closed his eyes and took a deep breath. He was ready. He'd never been more ready for anything.

After changing his clothes, he went downstairs to fetch his unopened gift in the living room. Tonight, they'd make a special memory of their own – opening their first Christmas gifts together. A peace offering. Spending the day with her, seeing her so happy, Garridan was determined to erase all the hurt he'd caused. From that moment on, all their memories would only be special.

Shelby tapped lightly on the door and pushed it open. Garridan was lying on the bed, listening to a heartrending rock ballad playing on his phone. He watched her as she walked towards him and she trembled under the intensity of his gaze. When she stood beside him, he threaded his fingers through hers and pulled her closer.

She resisted. "Come with me," she said, feeling uneasy about holding his hand so intimately there.

"Is everything okay?" he asked, sitting up and turning off the music.

"Yes. It's just that this was Daniel's room and it feels weird being with you like this in here."

He nodded. "Let's go."

She crossed the hall to her room, Garridan in tow, and closed the door behind them before joining him on her bed where he sat crossed-legged in the centre. He patted the space in front of him and she edged onto the bed, facing him. He placed their gifts between them.

"What's going on?" she asked and smiled when he took her hand in his.

"Opening gifts, of course. Today was great but I wanted us to have our own special moment. Just us," he said, caressing the back of her hand with his thumb.

"Okay," she sighed. Garridan moved her in so many ways.

"Maybe, if I'm lucky, it could become our tradition. We'd open our gifts on Christmas night instead of the morning," he said, looking hopeful.

Shelby swallowed. The pictures Garridan painted were so alluring, so tempting, she just wanted to say yes to everything. She wished she had a magic wand she could wave and everything that stood in their way would just disappear as if it never existed. She didn't know what to say, so she just sat there looking at him.

After a beat, he leaned in suddenly and kissed her. It was slow at first. Soft, gentle, tentative. She melted into him. She returned his kiss. Willingly. Eagerly. And then, as if she'd given him license, he pulled her against him and kissed her hungrily. His mouth possessed hers then moved across her jaw, her neck, and back to her mouth. It felt so right. So amazing. She didn't want it to end. It was wrong, so wrong. Warning bells sounded in the back of her mind. But she ignored them. She wanted this. She wanted him. Why couldn't she have him?

Because he's someone else's, her conscience replied.

Shelby shoved back against Garridan's chest, breaking their kiss. He looked confused, but the fire that burned for her was alive in his eyes.

"Garridan, we can't," she said breathlessly.

"I'm sorry," he said, wiping a hand across his face. "We need to talk."

She recoiled at his choice of words but agreed, "Yes, we need to talk."

GARRIDAN

Garridan worked to control his breathing. His body had responded to their kiss, so it was hard for him to focus just yet. He closed his eyes and pinched the bridge of his nose. Focus, he thought. It didn't help that he could still hear Shelby's ragged breaths beside him. But he had to get it together if he wanted to break the barrier between them.

When he finally regained control, he looked at her. She was watching him intently. Her face was flushed and her hair hung loosely over her shoulders. She was so beautiful. It's no wonder he couldn't resist her.

"I'm sorry, Shel. I shouldn't have done that. It's just so hard being this close to you and not being able to do any-thing about my feelings."

"What *do* you feel, Garridan? I really need to know what's going on because I can't stand this anymore."

"What do you want to know?"

She exhaled. "I want to know about the things we didn't speak about – personally, your work, Kimber. But I think you need to understand something about me first." She took his hand in hers. "I live my life hiding, shielding my-self from the outside world. I cocoon myself in my own little space where I control what happens, and the only people I let in are those who were here today."

He nodded. "You told me before, but I could tell by watching you today why you're so guarded about your life.

That's why I promised to protect you from the 'evils' of mine." He made air quotes and shrugged at his description.

"Yes, but I made a mistake," she countered. "When we met, I wanted to pull you into my little safe zone and ignore everything else. I thought the only thing that mattered was you as a person; that your life as a celebrity didn't matter because it isn't who you really are. But I was wrong. Your fame is such a big part of your life that it's impossible to ignore. How could I understand and love you completely if I didn't know the other side of you?"

"Is that why you said you didn't stalk me?"

"Yes and no," she said pensively. "Yes because of how social media distorts things, and no because I was terrified of seeing you with someone else."

He frowned. "But we hadn't met yet."

"The thought still hurt, Garridan," she sighed. "Long ago, after yet another breakup, I decided to tell all men who flirted with me that I was in a relationship. It was a lie I used to repel them; to stop them from pursuing me. But it had to feel real to me in order to be convincing – there had to be a name, a face, a personality – and because I already admired you, I created my fantasy man based on Sergeant Jameson – on *you* – and built on it. And the more I pretended, the more real it felt." She picked at her nail polish and looked mortified having to confess it but continued, "I knew you weren't married but when I realised I've never seen you with a woman, every night I'd say 'wait for me' hoping that by some miracle, you actually would. And then I hoped that by another miracle, we'd meet and you'd fall madly in love with me and we'd live happily ever after in our cocoon."

Garridan smiled at the image she created and was surprised at how deeply she felt for him even before they'd met. But their relationship is something he had to admit would probably not have happened if he hadn't noticed her first. He meets beautiful women every day – fans – and it would be easy for him to date any of them. But he didn't date fans apart from a few reckless mistakes. Like most public figures, he'd meet women through friends, at work, or even at events. But they'd always be other celebrities. Not fans.

"If you saw me before I noticed you, would you have approached me? As a fan?" he asked.

"I don't know," she shrugged, looking sceptical. "I see famous people all the time here and I've never approached any of them. I also have friends who are celebrities – actors, sports stars – but when I see them, it's like seeing a friend, not a famous person. I honestly don't know what I would've done if I saw you first."

Again, Garridan was surprised. From what she'd told him, it seemed as if she was taken by him for a long time. But knowing that she probably wouldn't have approached him, explained so much about her respect of privacy and personal space. And realising that he might not have met her if one small event didn't work in their favour that day, he was grateful he'd seen her first.

"So what would you have done if we hadn't met?" He was very curious to know what her Plan B was. He imagined another man in his place, sharing that moment with her. He didn't like it very much.

She shrugged as if it was obvious. "Be alone forever."

That took Garridan's breath away. He couldn't understand why. Why would someone with so much love to give want to be alone forever?

"Why?" he asked.

"Because I don't want to get hurt anymore. And that's all loving someone causes," she replied, averting her eyes. "I've tried enough times to know the inevitable outcome."

Now he understood. It's not that she didn't want to love; it's that men didn't know how to love her. Anyone in their right mind would know to treasure her if they were lucky enough to have her.

"And what about me? Will loving me cause you pain?"

She looked at him sadly. "It already has."

SHELBY

Garridan's sad expression tugged at Shelby's heart. She didn't want to hurt him in any way, but she had to be honest. They promised to talk, to bare it all, and she did.

Her heart hammered as she waited while he processed everything she'd just told him. She cringed inwardly as she recalled her confession and hoped he wasn't thinking about fleeing on account of her delusions. Saying it out loud made her sound like a lunatic, even to herself – a grown woman harbouring romantic fantasies like an enamoured teenager. But it was all said and done now, and what Garridan did with it was out of her control.

She adjusted her posture and sat up straight, pretending to don an invisible armour and prepared herself for the outcome – whatever it might be.

The way his gaze penetrated her was unnerving. She wondered what he was thinking. He ran a hand through his hair and rubbed his neck. Sometimes when he did that, Shelby got the feeling his hand automatically continued further down to his neck because that's what it did when he wore his hair longer to suit a particular role.

"Garridan?" she prodded.

"Can we get some drinks?" he asked suddenly.

"Sure. Anything," she said.

They walked together quietly to grab a few things from the kitchen. She was glad he suggested it because getting out of the room eased some of the tension she was feeling.

When they returned, they sat back against the headboard, a drink in hand. After a few sips, he turned to face her. He looked ready to talk.

"Before we speak about my work, I think I should clear up the Kimber situation," he said, eyeing her. "Because I really want to hold you in my arms and kiss you without you freaking out again," he added matter-of-factly.

"Okay," she giggled. Shelby couldn't help laughing at Garridan's flippant comment, but even in the lightness of their mood, hearing Kimber's name caused a knot to form in her stomach.

He inhaled deeply and his eyes danced across the room as if he was wondering where to begin. "I met Kimber at a fashion show. A friend of mine invited me, and Kimber was one of the models."

Wow, Shelby thought. No competition. "Is that what she's famous for?" she asked, trying not to sound intimidated.

"Yes. She's a model. Well, at least she was one until I met her. That was her last night on the runway before retirement," he said, shaking his head. "It was just before her twenty-eighth birthday two years ago."

"So you were together for two years?"

"No, we bumped into each other again early this year and I asked her out. And that was where it all began. After her retirement, she struggled to secure modelling jobs and her self-esteem took a serious knock. She was losing more and more followers, and needed to bolster her reputation. I think I was her way in. She also has a hang-up about being considered too old for some of the events she used to have exclusive access to. When we were together, she'd always do things to look younger. It was hard for me to get to know her as a person because she was always so preoccupied with what everyone else thought about her."

Shelby listened quietly as Garridan told her that when his feelings for Kimber didn't grow, she did things to win his favour, which then graduated to her manipulating him publicly and eventually becoming obsessed with him.

"And it pushed me away. I called it off between us, and that's when she flipped out," he said.

"In what way?"

"Everything you've seen – in person, on social media, the news – it's all part of Kimber's grand plan to make me hers."

"So you're not getting married?"

Her question surprised him and she reminded him about the interview.

"You saw that, huh? No, we're not getting married. We're not even in a relationship."

Shelby exhaled softly as the weight she felt was lifted. "And the baby?" she asked.

"The baby is real. Due in February. But I don't know if it's mine and I won't accept responsibility until I do."

"Why do you say that? Weren't you her last boyfriend?"

"I suppose I was, officially. But Kimber did things to get my attention. I guess in her way, she thought that if she slept with other men, I'd get jealous and she'd win me back."

"Were you jealous?"

"Not at all," he replied without hesitation. "I tried to

make it work but if I think back, I hardly felt anything real for her beyond initial attraction." He paused for a bit, then said, "I do get jealous when I think of *you* with someone else." He looked at her lovingly and brushed a strand of hair behind her ear.

"But I'd never do anything like that. You're the only man I don't avoid."

"I know. And I love you even more for it." He kissed the palm of her hand. "But back to Kimber. She agreed to a DNA test."

An emotion passed briefly across Garridan's face and Shelby noted something different in his voice.

"You sound sad about it," she said.

He nodded but avoided her eyes. "I am. When we spoke about you not wanting more kids, a child was the furthest thing from my mind. I didn't even know how to answer your question. But now that the possibility of me becoming a dad exists, I'm growing excited. I actually want it. But when I remember it might not be mine, I get sad."

This changes things. Would Garridan want to rekindle things with Kimber if the baby is his? And if it isn't, would he want to be with Shelby knowing how she felt about having more kids? Would he try to change her mind now that he knows he wants a child? Shelby would give anything to be with him except have a child. Will this be the one thing they wouldn't find a solution to? Will it drive them apart forever?

He must've noticed something in her expression because he asked, "Are you okay?"

She didn't answer because she wasn't okay. Was it even

necessary to continue this if, in the end, it didn't matter? What was the point of them fixing things if it wasn't going to change anything? She decided not to distance herself yet. She still had unanswered questions.

"What about the party on my last night in Miami? And the following day at the airport?"

"The picture Kimber posted was from a party earlier this year. Long before we met."

"So why post it in July and make it look like you guys were together that night?" Shelby asked, appalled.

He shrugged. "I have no idea. She usually does things like that. At the time, I assumed she wanted to cause a rift between us but when I confronted her, she said it was just a memory she wanted to post."

"So where were you?"

With a faraway look in his eyes, he told Shelby why he didn't make it for their last date and arrived late to the airport the following day. He also told her how he and Rodrigo watched as the plane took off.

"Didn't Harlow tell you about that?" he asked. "I know the two of them were always in contact."

"She tried, I guess, but I didn't want to hear anything about you."

"I vowed to fix things between us, but you didn't make it easy. I had no way of contacting you to explain."

"You only had the temporary number I used while we were in the U.S., so I forbade Harlow from giving Rodrigo the one I use here. I had a feeling you'd ask."

"I did ask. But I also messaged you privately on social media, and sent emails to the address I found on your website. But suddenly I couldn't find your social media accounts anymore and I wasn't sure my emails were reaching you. It was like you just disappeared. I felt so lost. I knew nothing about your life here. Rodrigo was my only connection to you, but I could sense his anxiety all the way from L.A., so I stopped bugging him. After a while, I assumed you'd moved on with someone else." He laughed without humour.

"Did *you* move on?" she asked, but she wasn't sure she wanted to know the answer.

His eyes burrowed into hers. "No. You were all I could think of. We filmed in Spokane and that distracted me a little but you were never far from my mind." He stroked her cheek. "I couldn't even eat or sleep properly. I was a mess."

"And now you're here," she said.

What happens now? Things can't just go back to normal like there wasn't something that threatened their future. No matter what, she still wasn't prepared to have a baby for him.

"And now I'm here." Garridan said and pulled her into his arms.

Her back was against his chest. He could tell she was processing what he'd told her but she was also overthinking things. He sensed her trepidation about him wanting a child. But he didn't want to waste another minute of their time together. Listening to their individual stories just proved how senseless they'd been. Separated all those months because they chose not to speak about what was really going on, and basing their decisions and actions on pure speculation. They were no better than the tabloids.

"What are you thinking?" she asked.

"About how we wasted time when we should've been together. And how I don't want any more time to slip through my fingers."

"So what's next?" she asked, turning to face him.

"I really want us to try again. I tried, but I can't live without you." The ache he felt the past few months hadn't disappeared completely yet. He never wanted to feel that lost ever again.

"I was miserable without you," Shelby said as sadness crossed her features momentarily. "I also want to try, but there are so many things to consider."

"I know you're worried about Kimber and how I feel about the baby. I can tell by the way you tense up when we speak about it."

She nodded. "It *is* something that bothers me. A lot. It's a big deal, Garridan."

She was right. He had no doubt it was something they'd have to deal with along the way, but he wasn't going to give up just yet. He was determined to make things work. He'd do whatever it takes.

"It's a big deal. But can we at least try being together first before we think that far ahead?"

She nodded slowly as she considered his suggestion. "Okay," she finally agreed. "But as long as you know where I stand on this. And we have to think things through this time. We can't just rush every decision based on our feelings."

"Okay," he nodded. He could live with that. "No more rash decisions."

"Thank you," she smiled.

Garridan could see her relief. He was relieved too. He didn't know what he would've done if she'd said no.

"Thank you," he said, smiling back at her. "Now?" he asked.

She frowned. "Now what?"

"Can I now finally kiss you?"

He didn't wait for her reply. He pinned her to the bed and planted kisses all over her face, causing her to laugh.

She wiggled out of his grasp. "Nope, no kisses. Look at the time," she said, pointing at the clock.

"Ten thirty-two?" he asked. "Is it bedtime?"

She laughed and shook her head. "It's nearly tomorrow and we haven't opened our gifts."

They sat side by side. Shelby waited as Garridan unwrapped his gift, so they could open the boxes at the same time. When they lifted the lids, they both gasped.

Garridan carefully removed the timepiece from the box. It was stunning. A large analogue face, the background and straps deep brown with gold accents. There were several dials and gears, and a compass around the frame. He loved it. He looked over at Shelby who was stroking the delicate chains of her bracelet, handling it as if it were the most precious thing on Earth.

"It's symbolic of my endless love for you," he said when she looked up at him with a loving smile.

"I love it," she said, running the pad of her thumb over the infinity symbol that passed through a tiny heart. "It's perfect. Thank you, Garridan."

He smiled. "You're welcome." He leaned forward and put it on her wrist, placing a gentle kiss on her palm. "And I love mine." He held up the watch. "I don't even know what to say. Thank you."

"I have a confession to make," she said shyly.

"What is it?"

"It wasn't supposed to be a Christmas gift." She raised her brows as if to say sorry.

"I wondered how you managed to pull it off," he laughed.

She joined him. "I saw it soon after I returned home from Miami, so I got it for your birthday."

"Why didn't you send it to me?"

"Because I remembered what happened," she said, looking down as if the memory still hurt.

He pushed a gentle finger under her chin and tipped her head up. "Look at me."

She did.

"It would've made things better sooner, but I'm thankful for what we have now," he said, kissing her forehead affectionately.

"Did you read the inscription?" she asked.

"No, I didn't." He frowned and turned the watch over. Engraved on the back cover in tiny, delicate script was:

No matter the distance
No matter the time
Carry me in your heart
You'll always have mine

Garridan could only stare at it. His heart overflowed with love and appreciation for Shelby. He could see the correlation between the watch, their situation and the words. It was absolutely perfect.

"Thank you, baby," he said, taking her into his arms. "God I love you."

He expressed his love in the warmth of his gaze, the passion in his kiss, the tenderness of his caress, the declaration of her name, and the heavenly heights they climbed together.

In that moment, there was no one and nothing between them. In that moment, she knew she'd never loved anyone as much as she loved him.

"What was your favourite role?" Shelby asked.

They'd been lying in each other's arms – her head on his chest – for hours, talking about anything and everything, getting to know the other side of one another.

"I enjoyed them all on their own merit," he replied. "I got to be someone completely different for a short while. But I appreciate my role in the Ultimate Combatants movies because it brought me to myself. I don't know if that makes sense. It's as if I was lost and when they included me, I finally knew my place in the world. And once I found that place, it was like life began."

Shelby nodded. She knew what it was like to just float around, directionless, and not really belong anywhere.

"And the most challenging?"

"Being an abusive husband," he said without hesitation. "It was very difficult for me to get out of my head at first. It was emotionally draining. But I did a lot of research and even spent time with a man who'd killed his wife – the one the movie was based on. It was a horrific, eye-opening experience."

Shelby could imagine how hard it must've been. The characters Garridan played were so diverse, he definitely wasn't one-dimensional. His portrayal of the murderous ex-husband was so convincing that Garridan had received an award for it. But she'd never considered the emotional effect it would have on him.

"Do you have any regrets?" she asked.

"Not regrets. Lessons. Each role taught me something I didn't know about myself. It pushed me beyond what I thought were my limits." He paused as he took a deep, contemplative breath. "There were sad moments, though. Like Dominic's death. He was a great man and a brilliant actor. He left this world too soon. Things like that make me question a lot."

Shelby recalled the man who starred alongside Garridan in a dramatic action movie. His tragic passing after a long battle with cancer stunned the world. Sensing Garridan's sorrow, she held him close. "I'm really sorry, my love," she said, not knowing how else to comfort him.

"Thank you," he sighed and squeezed her in his arms as if he was drawing strength from her.

They continued their questioning until there was nothing left to ask about, and settled into a comfortable silence. As they lay, he drew lazy circles on her bare shoulder, his fingers going around and around on her skin. The sensation, paired with his even breathing, was soothing and entrancing, and it soon lulled her into a deep, peaceful sleep.

Shelby woke to the sound of her phone ringing. Half-asleep, she reached for it and answered with a croaky, "Hello?"

"Shel?" Harlow's voice came from the other side. "I'm sorry to wake you but this couldn't wait." The background was noisy and she sounded agitated.

Shelby sat up and turned on the bedside lamp. "What's wrong?" she whispered as she slipped into Garridan's t-shirt.

"I don't exactly know what's going on, but Kimber ran into us at the airport and she was so angry."

Shelby rolled her eyes at the mention of Kimber's name.

"She asked if Garridan was with you and when I said no, she accused me of lying and said she's going public with Garridan's and your secrets," Harlow's voice rose over the din.

"Wait, hold on. What secrets?"

Panic set in and Shelby shook Garridan awake while she listened to Harlow. She didn't have any secrets, but she worried about Garridan more. His entire career and public image rode on his reputation. Kimber was unstable and desperate, and one thing Shelby's learnt is that desperate people can be very dangerous. Who knew what Kimber would cook up?

"I have no idea," Harlow replied. "But if you know where Garridan is, please tell him. Or tell Quincy. Rodrigo tried, but couldn't reach him."

Damn! They still had a surprise proposal to protect. Shelby couldn't let that slip. As Garridan sat up next to her rubbing his eyes, she put her index finger over his lips. Harlow would be suspicious if she knew he was there.

"Thanks, Harlow," she said, letting him know who was on the phone. "I'll see if I can get hold of him."

"Okay. I gotta go. Love you and Merry Christmas!" Harlow said hurriedly, cutting the call before Shelby could respond.

The clock on her phone indicated it was three forty-one. They hadn't even slept for two hours. Shelby looked over at Garridan who was now wide awake.

"What's wrong?" he asked, frowning.

She sighed loudly and flopped dramatically onto the pillows. "Your baby mama."

Garridan recoiled and asked, "Kimber? What happened? Is it the baby?" He jumped up from the bed and looked frantically around the room. "Where's my phone?"

"Garridan, calm down." It both touched and concerned her that he was so worried. "The baby's fine. Kimber is acting out again. On second thought, I shouldn't even have woken you." Shelby's initial panic changed to anger. She looked at Garridan.

"You're glaring at me," he said, scowling at her as he snapped the elastic waist of his pyjama pants against his skin. "What did Kimber do?"

"She always finds a way to ruin the day. Not even thirteen thousand kilometres can stop her," Shelby fumed. "She's threatening to go public with our secrets," she said dryly, getting out of bed too.

"What secrets? We don't have secrets!" he said incredulously as he sat on the chair at her dressing table.

She threw her hands into the air and paced the room. "What does it matter if we have secrets or not? She'll make something up! No one actually gives a damn if it's true as long as there's a story!"

Shelby had listened to Garridan's version of his experience with Kimber, and she absolutely hated that he allowed her to do whatever she wanted while he just sat back saying 'that's what she does'. Here she was, worried about his career and reputation when all this time it didn't bother him.

What was he going to do about it? If he didn't care about himself, would he at least care about what happened to her? Or was he just going to allow her to be humiliated again? He was supposed to be protecting her from the 'evils' of his world as he put it, but every time Kimber was involved, he did nothing.

"What do you want me to do?" he yelled. "Everyone knows what she's like!"

Shelby grimaced. "Everyone knows, yet everyone buys it! They entertain it. Condone it! Do you think it's fair that she's dragging me into this mess now? And what am I supposed to do? Just suck it up?"

"Quincy's been handling things," Garridan said dismissively. "He's the PR guy and I trust him to fix this."

"Quincy is on vacation, Garridan! You can do something about this before it even happens – proactive versus reactive," she said sarcastically. "The only person who should be handling Kimber is you! You, Garridan!" She pointed at him. "You can't allow her to do this. If you don't do something about it, I will!"

His eyebrows flew towards his hairline. "Really? And what exactly are *you* gonna do?"

Shelby flinched at the contempt in his tone. "More than *you* apparently!" she shot back, spitting out the word 'you'. "What? Am I not famous enough? Not powerful enough? Not American enough to defend my name against the mighty Kimber Allyn, supermodel and baby mama of the equally-mighty Garridan Luca?"

Her breath was ragged and her heart drummed against her chest. She didn't *want* to be a bitch. But in that moment, she meant to be one. He deserved it. Why would he defend his psychotic, stalker ex-girlfriend when she was clearly trying to ruin his life, and Shelby's?

Garridan took deep, calming breaths. This was not what he wanted for them. They weren't the couple who yelled and insulted each other. He already had that with Kimber and he wouldn't allow her twisted games to ruin what he and Shelby had.

He walked over to Shelby and placed his hands on her shoulders massaging them gently. "Baby, I'm sorry. I didn't mean to insult you."

She wouldn't look at him but at least she wasn't pushing him away. She covered her face with her hands but he could tell she wasn't crying, so he just kept rubbing her shoulders, hoping it was easing some of the tension.

"I'm sorry too," she said eventually. "I'm just so tired of Kimber and all the drama she brings. I just want it to end so we can move on." She looked up at him, placing her hands over his on her shoulders. "And if she can't be handled, then I don't think I'll be able to be with you, Garridan."

His stomach twisted. It felt as though he'd been kicked in the gut. She'd leave him because of Kimber?

"I'm not used to this," she elaborated. "This is spiteful and vindictive and plain-down psychotic. I don't know anyone who'd do the things Kimber does, and I never expected this to be my life. I've worked too hard for too long to protect my little world and to protect my family from all sorts of drama just to let a jealous, self-centred brat ruin it all."

Garridan's hands dropped to his sides. He just got her back and he was losing her again. But she was right. It's not fair that she'd become one of Kimber's targets. It's his fault once again for tolerating her tantrums to a point where she was now outright malicious. Something had to be done to put an end to it. He sighed and sat heavily on the edge of the bed.

Shelby stood close. "You okay?" she asked, the concern in her voice palpable.

He pulled her onto his lap. He had to be honest with her about this so that she could help him deal with Kimber. This was *their* fight now. He needed her strength because he didn't know if he could be strong enough on his own.

"Talk to me," she urged.

"I'm scared." He couldn't look at her. He feared her reaction just as much as he dreaded what he was about to tell her.

She cupped his chin in her hand and forced him to look at her. "What are you scared of?" she asked softly.

"I'm scared of losing the baby," he replied. His voice cracked and tears pricked his eyes. He'd been carrying this secret for so long, it felt good to finally tell someone.

"Oh, Garridan," she said, wrapping her arms around his shoulders and cradling him to her chest, rocking him. "No-one can just keep your child from you. There are laws and if the baby is yours, Kimber will have to abide by them."

All he could do was nod. He'd never felt as vulnerable

as he did at that moment. On the one hand, he could lose the love of his life and on the other, he could lose his child. No matter what he did, he stood to lose something. And no matter what the law said, if he retaliated against Kimber, she would do everything in her power to make him pay.

He wrapped his arms around Shelby's waist and held tightly onto her. He needed her to anchor him because if she didn't, it felt as though he could float away into nothingness.

As much as Shelby hated seeing Garridan so torn, she was glad he finally opened up to her. She now understood his trepidation when it came to Kimber.

She didn't blame him for feeling that way because she knew how some women used their children to punish their exes. It was a sadistic and heartless thing to do. She could now help Garridan put safeguards in place to prevent that from ever happening if the baby is his. There was no way she'd allow an innocent child to be used as a pawn. As she rocked him in her arms, a plan started formulating in her mind. She was sure it would work – hopefully it would.

Garridan stifled a yawn as he lifted his head from her chest and she suddenly felt exhausted too. They'd had a long and eventful day. They could figure the rest out in the morning.

"Let's go to bed," she said

He nodded and silently waited for her to stand. And when they got back into bed, they turned into each other – she, wrapped up in him – and fell asleep.

GARRIDAN

They were seated in the living room, finalising their plans. Since Harlow's call, much of their time was spent watching the news and social media for anything Kimber-related. So far, there was nothing. The plan was simple, but it had to be dealt with carefully because of Kimber's state of mind.

The first step had already been executed. Garridan called Kimber the day after her threat to check on her and the baby. To avoid aggravating her, he lied about where he was. She was hysterical, cried uncontrollably and begged him to go back home. He told her he'd be back the following week and they'd talk. Garridan hated that he had to speak to her. She mistook any form of contact as him caring for her. And in this case, it was merely to appease her long enough to prevent her from going ahead with her threat.

Their next steps could only be carried out once he returned to L.A. He would consult his lawyer and petition for a restraining order, and hopefully include a condition that would also prevent Kimber from discussing Garridan and anyone associated to him on any media platform.

Once the restraining order is in place, a contract between Garridan and Kimber would be drawn up in respect of the baby. Kimber would be required to seek professional help for her obsession; a DNA test would be conducted soon after the birth; and, if the baby is his, Kimber would agree to a co-parenting arrangement containing provisions that would suit both parents but for the benefit of the baby, including her ongoing counselling.

The final step would be setting the record straight. After the baby is born, Garridan would take to social media and quash all the speculation and rumours surrounding him and Kimber. He'd be to the point and give only the facts. Nothing else. Shelby was helping him with that part. All he had to do when the time was right is copy, paste and post.

"Do you think it will work?" she asked, suddenly looking sceptical.

"I don't know," he shrugged. "But we have to try."

"This is a curveball. There's a chance she'll see it as an attack, you know?"

He knew. "But I've already tried everything else."

Garridan reminded himself that it was necessary. In just over a month, a baby would be born and no child should be deprived of love or be exposed to an unhealthy environment. They were doing this for the good of everyone. He just hoped it would work.

While Shelby rechecked the words on the laptop screen, her phone rang. She held it up for Garridan to see who was calling. Harlow and Rodrigo had finally arrived that morning. Their stay at Shelby's house was delayed until after Rodrigo's proposal to prevent Harlow from seeing Garridan and becoming suspicious.

"Hey, you!" she answered pleasantly. "What's up?"

Harlow's shrieking was so loud, Shelby had to hold the phone away from her ear. She tapped her ring finger indicating that Harlow had called to tell her about the engagement. Garridan chuckled softly and watched Shelby while she spoke. She looked almost as ecstatic as Harlow appeared to be. When she was done with the call, she smiled brightly.

"She sounds excited," Garridan said when Shelby put her phone away.

"She is. She really deserves to be happy."

"Everyone deserves to be happy," he said and after a short silence, he asked, "Do you want to get married someday?"

She laughed. "Well my dream of being a blushing young bride was over long ago. But I guess if the right man asked and I knew it was a sure thing, I'd definitely say yes."

He smiled and kissed her cheek. "Speaking of saying yes, we have a surprise engagement party to get ready for."

* * *

The days following the engagement party all merged into one. Since Harlow knew Garridan was there, she and Rodrigo could finally stay at Shelby's house, and the four of them went sightseeing as much as they could between visiting relatives while they were in the country.

The highlight was when, on New Year's Eve, he stood on a cliff overlooking the city, watching a gorgeous fireworks display with Shelby in his arms. They were far away from the rest of the city's inhabitants, with the skyline spread far and wide below them. They excitedly counted down the seconds to the New Year and when twelve o'clock rolled in, he kissed her under the warm, starry South African sky. He felt like the king of the world.

All too soon, it was time to return to L.A. Harlow and Rodrigo left three days before Garridan's flight was scheduled, so it was only him and Shelby at the airport.

"I'm going to miss you," she said through a teary smile.

"Just three short weeks, then we'll be together again." He tried to sound unaffected but he swallowed against the knot in his throat.

"I know," she sniffed. "But it still hurts. I got so used to you being around and now I have to go back to that empty house."

His heart sank when it was time to board. "Come here," he said, pulling her into an embrace. He rested his chin on her head, blinking back his tears. When he couldn't delay any longer, he tilted her head and kissed her passionately, hoping it would tide them both over until she was in his arms again. "See you soon, my baby. I love you."

She nodded and silent tears streamed down her cheeks. Garridan could see how hard she was trying to keep it together.

"I love you, Garridan. Always," she choked out. She wrung his shirt in her hands and clung to him as though she didn't want to let him go.

And with one last kiss, he pried his shirt from her grasp and left.

Shelby felt the void as soon as she stepped through the door. The tears that had dried on her way from the airport started flowing again.

Before Garridan's arrival, she loved being alone. She often couldn't wait to come home to just unwind and do her own thing. But in the past week, she'd gotten used to him being around, and standing in the entrance hall now, the silence was overwhelming. She could smell his cologne that still clung to the air, and it felt as if he would walk out of the kitchen at any moment.

With a heavy sigh and an even heavier heart, she traipsed upstairs. It was still early enough to make something to eat but she had no appetite, so she decided on a bath and some TV before trying to get some sleep.

Her throat tightened as she walked past her bed to the bathroom and images of Garridan sprawled on the bed flooded her mind. She already knew she'd have trouble sleeping without him. But as she waited for the tub to fill, she thought about his words. Garridan was right, in just three weeks' time she'd see him again. She definitely had something to look forward to.

The problems with Kimber were always in the back of her mind, and she was once again reminded of them during the holidays when she and Harlow had some time alone.

"So, what's up, Shel? Are you two official now?" Harlow

asked one day when Garridan and Rodrigo were out with the men of their family.

"I don't know, to be honest," Shelby replied. "We're trying. I want it more than anything but something's holding me back. I think it's all this uncertainty surrounding Kimber."

Harlow nodded, twirling her engagement ring around her finger. "It *should* worry you. You don't even know half of what's going on over there. Almost every day there's some news about them. It's a shit storm. And I know you probably don't want to hear this but, if you keep Garridan in your life, be prepared for constant drama."

That was exactly what Shelby feared. "We have a plan. Garridan will put everything in place when he gets back home."

"I hope it's a very good plan because that woman doesn't seem the type to take no for an answer."

But for once, the apprehension surrounding Kimber was overshadowed by something exciting – the thought of being with Garridan again soon, and also helping Harlow with her wedding.

As soon as they returned to the U.S., Harlow applied for a fiancé visa. After its approval, they'd have only three months in which to get married. Naturally, Harlow enlisted Shelby's help with everything she'd need from South Africa and Shelby would also travel to Miami to help finalise the preparations for the wedding. Their arrangements coincided with Shelby's birthday, so she decided to spend her birthday week with Garridan at his home in Los Angeles before going to Miami to help Harlow.

Thinking about something positive lifted her spirits and although Garridan's absence screamed at her through the silence, her heart felt lighter as she started wishing the days away.

Her lightheartedness faded gradually in the weeks that followed. Shelby found it harder and harder to remain positive, and she avoided her home because that's where she and Garridan had spent the most time together. It was where every corner, every sound, every smell reminded her of him.

She started doing things she hadn't done in the past – brunch and lunch with long-lost friends, movies twice a week, shopping. Anything to pass the time. But whatever she did, she made sure she was home for Garridan's call.

Because of the time difference and their work schedules, they agreed he should call her every day at eleven the morning, L.A. time, which allowed her to get home from a busy day and have supper before he called.

"I still wake up looking for you," he said one day during a video call. He looked weary.

Shelby knew exactly what he meant because she did the same thing. But she tried to comfort him instead, "Just one more week and we'll be together again."

Technology was an amazing tool, and Shelby was grateful they were able to keep in touch and never miss a beat of each other's lives. But it also made her feel lonely. She'd never been lonely before. Even when her kids all finally moved out, she missed them and was alone all the time but she never felt lonely. Until then.

Being away from Garridan also bred doubt and, sometimes, paranoia. At times, she questioned his love for her or his devotion – not outright, but to herself when she lay in bed, unable to sleep because her mind was too busy. She also wondered about him and Kimber. What if he changed his mind about her? What if they were spending time together?

"Cut it out!" she scolded herself on one particularly difficult night.

She knew her mind was playing tricks on her but she wasn't strong enough to ward off the destructive thoughts. In those times, she'd think about Kimber and feel sorry for her because she finally – maybe – understood why Kimber behaved the way she did.

By the time she was flying to L.A., Shelby was ready for Garridan to ask her to live with him. She didn't want to spend another day without him. When they were in Miami, it was the only thing he wanted. She even said she'd stay with him without knowing what his plan was, and it was something exciting they both looked forward to until she changed her mind. But he hadn't raised it with her again. Not once since they'd been back together, has he asked her to stay with him.

GARRIDAN

Garridan spotted Shelby as she cleared the security checkpoint. She chewed her bottom lip as she scanned the waiting area expectantly. He crossed the room when her gaze met his, and couldn't help but smile when relief washed over her features.

"Hey, beautiful," he said, swooping her into his arms. "I missed you so damn much!"

She wrapped her arms around his neck and clung tightly. "Hi, handsome," she replied as he pecked her cheek and took her bags.

"Welcome to Los Angeles! How was your flight?"

"Too long. But I'm so glad I'm finally here," she smiled, looking up at him.

Garridan had been looking forward to Shelby's visit and even though they'd spoken every day since he arrived back home from South Africa, nothing felt better than having her right there with him. She planned to stay for just a week and although it wasn't nearly long enough, he was grateful she sacrificed time she could've invested in her work to spend it with him while she was in the country to help Harlow.

They walked hand in hand in silence, and when he looked down at her, he noticed her glancing uneasily at the passing crowd. He realised she'd become aware of the stares and whispers around them. The attention was so much a part of his life that he didn't notice it anymore, but her expression forced him to look at it from her perspective. It was very intrusive.

"How's Kimber?" she asked suddenly, not looking at him. Her hand tightened around his.

"Stable," he replied, unable to think of a more appropriate way to describe his ex's irrational and uncontrollable mood swings.

He then realised the reason behind Shelby's unease. It wasn't that people were staring at them; it was that Kimber would get wind of her being there and with him.

"I spoke to her about you coming, babe. She has no choice but to understand," he offered, but she continued looking around nervously. "You'll be with me all the time, okay? I won't let anything happen to you."

Garridan and his team had been hard at work planning for the year ahead. He had two busy months of interviews, screenings, and everything else Marc and Quincy had scheduled. A lot of it required travelling but thankfully, none of his travels would take place in the week of Shelby's visit. That meant she could join him the entire time. It wasn't ideal, but he'd rather have her with him throughout the day than wait alone until he returned home to her at night.

"Okay," she said. "I'm sorry. I just don't want any problems."

"There won't be." He squeezed her hand reassuringly.

He didn't think Kimber was a threat because she'd accepted the conditions of their agreement and, according to one of Quincy's sources, had been doing well since her regular therapy sessions.

Garridan updated Shelby when each step of their plan had been carried out. At the time, she seemed relieved that everything went well and didn't once mention any concerns. But perhaps being in the country and so close to Kimber was causing some doubt.

It was a cloudy afternoon and on the drive home, Shelby had her window down slightly, the breeze playing in her hair. Garridan couldn't wait to get home and catch up with her, but she seemed distracted. She'd been staring pensively out of the window and hadn't said a word since the airport.

"You're quiet," he said.

She stretched and inhaled deeply. "I think I'm a little tired. Sorry," she said, reaching out and taking his hand in hers.

He looked down at their fingers interlaced on his lap and pulled her hand to his lips, kissing it gently. He missed her little touches.

"We'll be home in a bit. After we have lunch, you can rest while I make some calls, okay? We'll catch up tonight."

"That sounds great, thank you," she smiled and brushed her thumb across his knuckles.

"I hope you're ready for your birthday?" he said, looking at her mischievously.

"Why?" She screwed her eyes. "What are you planning?" she asked suspiciously.

He smiled.

"Did I ever tell you I don't like surprises?" she mumbled.

He laughed because all he ever did was surprise her. "I love surprising you. It's my favourite thing to do," he said, his eyes leaving the road briefly to glance at her. She was looking at him with the adoration he loved so much.

"Yeah, I noticed that," she laughed. "I'm ready...as long as you're part of the surprise," she said, waggling her brows like he always did.

Garridan chuckled at her playfulness. "Baby, I'm the biggest part."

It'd been a while since Shelby pinched herself to make sure Garridan was really in her life, but she did it as she walked through the door. She couldn't believe she was in his house. She was staying with him. She was finally there.

He playfully carried her over the threshold like he did at the cabin. She laughed at his silliness, but was soon cut off when he finally pulled her into a passionate kiss that took her breath away. She swooned a little when he released her.

"I couldn't wait to do that," he said in a low voice, crouching to look into her eyes, his hands cupping her neck. "Let's get you settled."

He led her by the hand, showing her the different rooms. When they reached his bedroom, he referred to it as 'our bedroom' and there was a fire in his eyes. He was clearly just as affected by their kiss as she was. It caused little flips in her stomach.

Something had changed inside her since their time together in Johannesburg. Something about her feelings for him and what she now hoped for. The past six years had only been a fantasy, and the last few weeks without him had been torture. Both times, all she yearned for was him, only in different ways. But now, being there, she wanted more. She wanted forever with him. And for the first time since they'd met, she was scared she'd never really have him.

"I'll be downstairs in the study if you need me," he said after lunch, kissing her forehead before he left the room so she could rest.

She lay on the bed and although she was exhausted, she couldn't settle down. What was she going to do about these feelings? Given Garridan's history with clingy and needy, she was afraid that what happened to Kimber would happen to her. She didn't feel clingy or needy, but she did feel a deep-rooted love that she wanted to explore without the distance. There was no way he would move to South Africa to be with her and there was no hope for them if they stayed apart. The only solution would be for her to move to L.A. to be with him. But is that still what he wanted? Would he be ready for what it would mean for them?

And then there was Kimber. Shelby had forgotten what it was like to be so close to the woman who threatened their happiness, and walking through the airport was a harsh reminder of what being with Garridan would mean for her. Apart from the intrusive gawking, she didn't like that Garridan had discussed her arrival with Kimber. If he asked her to stay, would Kimber have a say? How would Garridan deal with her ever-constant presence? He said Kimber had no choice but to understand that she was in the country, but what would he have done if she didn't understand?

Shelby tossed and turned as the doubts and fears and questions replayed in her mind until she eventually fell asleep.

Shelby was in a much better mood after her nap. Garridan had worried that something was wrong. He actually thought she was having doubts about being with him, which distracted him all afternoon while he tried to wrap up some business so he could spend her birthday with her the next day.

While he waited for her to shower and get ready for their evening out, he marvelled at their relationship. He still couldn't believe she was there.

It was strange because when he thought about it, although they knew each other for six months, they'd been separated for five of those months and only spent real time together for a total of two weeks. Normally, a brief encounter on a vacation would've left him with a faint memory, but with Shelby it was different. The thought of her not being in his life distressed him, and some irrational part of him felt as though she could change her mind at any moment and leave him with the emptiness he felt when they were apart. He couldn't allow it. If she loved him as much as he loved her, he wasn't going to allow what happened the last time to happen again. He wasn't going to let their doubts, fears and distance break their bond. He needed to reassure her of his feelings for her. And he'd do it before she left for Miami.

The previous times they were together were over a holiday

period. They'd never had a simple, hassle-free night out since they'd met. This would be their first week together outside of holiday celebrations and family and friends. It was just the two of them and he wanted it to be both as normal and as special as possible. He wanted her to know what it could be like to live with him on a regular day, and also the lengths he'd go to to make her feel like the most loved woman in the world. Today was one of the normal as possible days.

"Where are we going?" she asked curiously as they drove along the busy street.

"Just dinner and a movie," he said, looking over at her. "That okay?"

The air was cool from the earlier drizzle and they both wore bomber jackets. With her ponytail, it felt like they were college sweethearts going on their first date.

"That's perfect. Thank you." She hesitated then asked, "But can we skip the movie, please?" She looked mortified, as if she was asking him to move a mountain.

"Of course. Anything you want."

"I think I'd just like to spend time with you. Catch up."

"I'd like that too. You okay with the restaurant, though? We can order in if you prefer."

She nodded. "The restaurant's good. Thank you."

It was one of Garridan's favourite places to escape to. People knew him there. Like family. No photos, no autographs. Just a great time and a great meal away from home. He couldn't take any of his exes there because their taste was a little different – he couldn't even imagine any of them wearing jeans and combat boots on a date to a restaurant. But he knew Shelby would love it. He knew she'd appreciate the reason he loved it.

They parked in the small lot and when she stepped out of the car, the smile on her face was radiant. He knew she'd love it.

The restaurant was amazing. Rustic. Garridan was the only man who'd ever really listened to Shelby when she spoke about the things she loved, so when she first saw it, she thought he'd chosen this place because of its architecture.

It was an old stone house that, together with the wet weather and smoke billowing from the chimney, resembled an old English country house from centuries before as depicted in story books. She didn't know where to look first. Every stone, every roof tile, the cobbled path, were all beautiful and added to the charm of the old place.

"Wow!" she said. "I love this, Garridan."

But when they stepped through the door, she could immediately tell he'd chosen it because of the atmosphere. Homely, cosy and intimate. There were no stares or interruptions and when they entered, they were greeted warmly as if they'd always belonged. It was exactly the type of place that would make Garridan feel at ease.

They were seated near the fireplace and instead of sitting across the table from her, Garridan sat to her left. He held her hand as they spoke, lazily massaging her fingers and palm as they caught up with everything they'd missed out on while they were separated.

"That must've been awkward," he laughed when she told him about a client who had flowers and chocolates delivered to her house.

She covered her face with her hand. "It was more embarrassing than awkward. I had to tell him about us but he wouldn't believe me," she laughed.

"I guess that's understandable," he chuckled. "What did you do for him?"

"An autobiography. It's still in progress," she said. "We met a few times so I could gather the information I need to write it. But he's a busy entrepreneur and I was always available to meet with him at short notice, and that was why he didn't believe me when I told him about us. The perils of ghostwriting," she said, laughing again.

Garridan didn't laugh. "I really think we need to make this official," he said with an earnest expression.

She took a sip of her hot chocolate, mostly to hide her astonishment at his sudden change in direction. "What do you mean?"

"I want us to be a real, official couple. I don't want this long distance, travelling-when-we-can thing anymore."

"I don't want it either, Garridan, but what else can we do? It's not like we have another choice." She had to dig deep to say those words when all she wanted to say was *Yes! I want that too!* But she couldn't.

"I also don't want anyone else flirting with you just because they don't know about us. You shouldn't have to prove our relationship. It should be obvious." He took both her hands in his and said, "Stay with me."

"I want to stay," she said honestly. "But there are things that worry me."

"What things?" he asked, frowning deeply.

"Kimber, for one. I don't want you to explain me to her.

You shouldn't have to. I understand your concerns and her issues, but we have nothing to do with her."

He nodded. "Fair enough. What else?"

"What is your plan exactly? I mean, how do you propose I stay with you. It's not like I can just pack up my life and move here."

This time, he smiled. "There's something that I'm waiting confirmation on before I can tell you, but I do have a plan," he said, kissing her knuckles.

Shelby couldn't help but wonder why things between them were always so complicated. When it came to them as a couple in their little bubble, things were smooth. Easy. But everything else around them and relating to them was one complication after another. She thought about Harlow and how things just fell into place once she and Rodrigo met. Now she wondered if she and Garridan would ever catch a break. As much as she loved him and wanted to be with him, whatever his plan was, she wasn't saying yes until she was completely sure she wouldn't be uprooting her entire life for nothing.

"Okay," she conceded. "I'll wait to hear your plan before I give you an answer."

He could practically see the gears turning in her head. Shelby was such a deep thinker and so guarded, Garridan hoped she wasn't trying to talk herself out of saying yes.

"Being with you and your family was one of the best times of my life. I hated being away from you after that – alone, sleeping without you. I couldn't stand it. And now that I know what it's like to have you in my house, I don't want you to leave."

This time, she kissed his hands. "I'm not saying no, Garridan. I really want what you want, but I have to be smart about this. For me. You know what I've been through and what led me to being a single mom. This time, I need to be sure about *me* so that I never have doubts about *you*."

He knew what she'd given up to be with her sons' father and how she sacrificed even more to raise her sons on her own. She truly did have to make the decision for her. Because of her.

"Okay, I agree. We'll talk about it more when I tell you my plan. Then you can take all the time you need to decide." He looked into her eyes. "Deal?"

"Deal," she said.

Her smile told him she was relieved and he wondered how long she'd been worrying about the things she'd just spoken about.

"Good. So let's forget about that for now. I don't know

about you, but I'm ready for dessert." He signalled the waiter.

"Yes, please," she laughed.

They spent the rest of the evening at the restaurant and at home talking, laughing and making up for lost time.

Garridan woke up early the following morning. Although it wouldn't be a long drive to her birthday surprise, he wanted them to eat a wholesome breakfast so they could have enough energy for the day. It wasn't anything extravagant but he was both excited and anxious to see her reaction.

He was also anxious about what he planned for later and asked his team to come over the evening to help them celebrate the proposal – if she said yes. He'd probably need them for moral support anyway if she said no, but he didn't want to think about that.

While he waited for the coffee to brew, his phone vibrated in his pocket. It was a message from Quincy: *You were spotted at the airport.* The picture attached was of Garridan and Shelby walking through the airport when she arrived. It was captioned: *Garridan Luca accompanies former girlfriend as she arrives in L.A.* Garridan sent a quick thank you in reply. He assumed there'd be at least one report about them and was happy to see it wasn't bad. No speculation or anything that would ruin Shelby's day.

He finished making the breakfast of eggs, sausages and toast, and poured coffee and orange juice. After setting everything up on a tray, he carried it to the bedroom where he added her gift and placed it on the small table next to the window before walking over to the bed to wake her. She was curled on her side with her knees folded into her chest and her hands tucked under her cheek.

"Happy birthday to you. Happy birthday to you," he sang off-key and rubbed her shoulders gently, and smiled when she opened her eyes. "Happy birthday to the love of my life. Happy birthday to you!"

"Good morning, Garridan," she smiled and sat up.

He brought the tray to the bed and sat next to her.

"Happy birthday, baby," he said, handing her a mug of coffee and lifting his to the air to make a toast. "May your day be perfect and may you be blessed with everything you've ever wanted."

They clinked mugs and he leaned in to kiss her.

"Thank you so much, Garridan." She looked at him lovingly. "I already have everything I've ever wanted."

He handed her the gift and his heart drummed against his chest. When he bought it, he thought it was perfect to complete the other pieces of jewellery he'd already given her. But now that she was carefully unwrapping it, he wasn't so sure anymore. It was a dainty ring – a garnet and emerald placed side by side and set in a simple gold band. He worried she'd read too much into it and scare herself off.

Shelby was looking down when she opened the box, so he couldn't see her expression. But after a few long seconds, she looked up and her lips curved into a slow smile.

"I love it," she said as she gently ran her finger over the delicate ring, tracing the stones. "My birthstones."

He nodded. "It reminded me of you. Petite, timeless and beautiful."

He watched as she took the ring from the box and placed it on the ring finger of her right hand.

"I hope it's not too much."

"It's beautiful. Thank you," she said, leaning in to embrace him.

"You're welcome." He kissed the top of her head. "Okay, birthday girl. Let's get going."

The day was cloudy and it would probably rain later. Shelby and Garridan chatted happily as he drove. He showed her the picture Quincy had sent and she was relieved the article wasn't gossip or speculation. It was just a picture of them holding hands at the airport and a simple, semi-accurate caption. It still felt strange to see her own face displayed so publicly, but she decided not to think about it too much and focused on the scenery around her.

"Are you still not going to tell me where we're going?" she asked as she looked through the window trying to find clues.

He smirked. "You're going to love it. And please don't guess because I won't be able to lie if you get it right."

She tried hard not to ask him because she didn't want to ruin the surprise. They'd never discussed her wish list or anything else about her birthday, so she was very curious about where he was taking her. But after about twenty minutes, he turned a corner and she nearly jumped out of her seat.

"What?!" she exclaimed when the main entrance came into view. She recognised it from pictures on the internet. "We're going to the adventure park?" she asked again, looking at Garridan for confirmation.

He looked almost as happy as she felt.

"Yep," he said as he parked the car. "Surprise!"

Shelby couldn't believe her eyes. It was something she'd

always wanted to do but never thought she actually would. And never in a million years did she think she'd be there with Garridan. She was still reeling by the time he opened her door, but she recovered when he tugged gently on her hand and led her out of the car.

"I don't even know what to say, Garridan! Thank you!" She flung her arms around his neck and kissed him. "How did you know?"

He shrugged. "You seem like the person who'd enjoy it here. You'd let your imagination run wild," he said, looking down at her where she stood in his arms.

"You have no idea how happy you've made me."

"You haven't even been inside yet," he laughed. "Let's go."

They spent the day exploring, enjoying the rides and everything there was to see. Shelby felt like a little girl in awe of the wonders of the place, carrying the souvenirs Garridan had bought for her. It was like a dream come true. Two dreams.

She thought about her past relationships and how none of them had come even close to what she and Garridan had. Although they hadn't been together long, he knew her well enough to know that she'd love this experience before she even mentioned it to him. Only those very close to her knew her desire, so it was a very unexpected and beautiful surprise.

The weather was kind and kept the rain at bay until shortly after two o'clock. They were making their way from one of the rides and were about to have lunch when it started drizzling. It was a light, steady drizzle that wasn't going to let up soon, so they headed back home. Garridan had something planned for later the night, and Shelby was happy they'd have some time alone before then.

The drive back was quiet, so she read and replied to the messages she'd received from some of her relatives and friends back home. The time difference meant they were already asleep but, thankfully, her sons and parents made a group video call to her before she and Garridan left his house that morning. Her heart swelled with love and gratitude for everyone who made her day special.

Her thoughts were never far from the morning's news about them. She realised once again that if she wanted a future with Garridan, she'd have to get used to seeing herself in some or other media report. She was bracing herself for the inevitability of their appearance there again soon, if they hadn't already made the news because of their day out.

Although she tried her best to ignore it, throughout the day, she noticed the stares, the nudges, and the sneaky photos Garridan had once told her about. It was easier to deal with now than it was at the airport the day before – probably because the story about them wasn't as bad as she thought it would be. She could imagine the headline: 'Garridan Luca and winter fling out having fun', and tried not to laugh at herself for feeling like a seasonal fruit. Still, the probability of Kimber reacting badly seemed to worry Shelby more than it did Garridan.

"What are you thinking?" Garridan asked as he parked in his driveway.

"Nothing much," she said, shaking her head. She didn't want to ruin their great day with her wayward thoughts. "Just thinking about today. I don't think I've ever been this spoilt."

"Well, it's not over yet," he grinned, before he walked around the car and opened her door.

Garridan's living room was alive with chatter and laughter that evening. The supper he'd planned was a success and everyone was now relaxing and enjoying drinks and each other's company. Garridan, Marc and Quincy debated their predictions about the future of the film industry while Shelby, Megan and Quincy's wife, Alyssa, were engrossed in their own discussion on the other side of the room.

Garridan checked his watch and winked at the guys. It was time. With a nervous twist in his stomach, he called Shelby over to him. The room grew silent as he met her halfway and placed an arm around her waist, pulling her close. He felt her tense and noticed a slight frown on her brow. She obviously hated that everyone's attention was on her. They stood in the middle of the room. Garridan faced Shelby and cleared his throat.

"Babe, as you know, Quincy and Alyssa's son is dyslexic, and he needs lots of one on one attention and help when it comes to his schoolwork." Shelby nodded in acknowledgement and Garridan continued, "Alyssa now has to spend more time with him and won't be able to manage my fan club, and my online and social media presence." He took a deep breath. "That's why I want to hire you to take over from her."

Shelby tensed again and her eyes grew wide. "You want me to *work* for you?" she asked and withdrew from him.

He stopped her from pulling away too far. "It's what Quincy suggested as a way of getting you to be with me. Like Harlow did when she moved here." Garridan's heartbeat spiked a little. "It would be easier for us to be together this way. I want you to stay with me. Please?" Shit! He should've done this in private.

"But I'm not qualified for that kind of work," she said.

"You have knowledge," he said, tapping her head lightly with his finger. "You're an amazing writer. You know me well, you know what my supporters want and you want what's best for me. You're the perfect choice. The only choice."

He could feel beads of sweat forming on his forehead. What if she said no? Garridan cupped his hands around Shelby's face and looked into her eyes.

"Please say yes," he said and didn't care if it sounded like he was begging. He needed her with him and he'd do anything for her to stay. "I love you and I need you more than you know. Please say yes."

"Well, isn't this cosy?" Kimber's maniacal voice came from the doorway leading to the living room.

Garridan's head whipped in that direction and three things happened at once: Marc and Quincy leapt from the couch and stood in front of Kimber, preventing her from entering the room; Megan and Alyssa stood protectively closer to Shelby; and, Shelby planted herself steadily into Garridan's side.

Garridan was fuming. "How did you get in, Kimber?"

Her wet hair clung to her face, her usually flawless

makeup was a swirled, colourful mess running down her cheeks and she was dripping puddles onto the floor.

She punched a fist into the air and showed him a key. "How else?!" she replied angrily, wiping a hand across her face, smearing her makeup further. "It's amazing what a piece of clay can do," she said smugly. "And I can't believe how easy it was. You barely look at me anymore, so I did it right here!" She pointed at Garridan's keys on the table behind her.

"Are you okay, Kimber?" Alyssa asked gently as if speaking to a child. "Can we get you anything?"

Kimber's eyes focused in on Garridan and Shelby. "Can you get her"–she pointed at Shelby with a look of hatred–"to leave my man alone?"

"I'm not your man!" Garridan yelled.

Shelby flinched beside him and he pulled her even closer.

"You're mine, Garridan!" Kimber raised her voice, "Mine!"

"Calm down, Kimber," Marc said as he placed a hand on her shoulder.

"No! Leave me alone!"

Kimber swiped at Marc and he lurched out of her reach.

"You're proposing to her?" she asked Garridan with a pained look in her eyes. "To *her*! Look at her! She's *nobody*! An old, insignificant nothing! What do you even see in her anyway?"

"Kimber, please," Garridan sighed, pinching the bridge

of his nose. "I've warned you about showing up here unannounced. You're not allowed to be here."

"I saw the way you looked at her when she danced for you," Kimber prattled on, ignoring his threat. "I saw the look in your eyes! It was more than lust. You *never* looked at me that way. Not even when *I* danced for you!" she snivelled and wiped her nose with the back of her hand.

"Is *that* why you posted that picture?" Garridan frowned. Why didn't he realise it before?

"*Everyone* was talking about her dancing for you. It was everywhere I looked. It got so many likes no matter who posted it. Did you see the comments? They love her. They *love* you," she said to Shelby, nodding wildly like a deranged bobblehead doll.

The air in the room was unnerving. Quincy and Marc held their divide between Kimber and everyone else. She paced back and forth in front of them, her gaze locked on Shelby. It reminded Garridan of a lion stalking its prey.

"You don't have to do this, Kimber," Garridan tried again to placate her. "Let me take you home."

"And then you took her to the adventure park," she said bitterly. "Who even cares about that anymore? But everybody loves that you took her. They think you're a cute couple." She scrunched her face when she said 'cute'.

"What the hell are you talking about?" Garridan was slowly losing his patience. He was so tired of her games.

"It's all over the internet," Alyssa said, looking down at her phone. She held it up for Garridan to see. "Your outing this morning is trending."

"You've never posted about *me*, Garridan! What does

she have that I don't?" Kimber hissed. Her features contorted when she faced Garridan.

"It's not ab–" Garridan started, but she cut him off.

"I'm the one who loves you!" She banged on her chest, bordering on hysterics. "I'm the one who's carrying your child!" Kimber's hands landed on her swollen belly as she screeched the words through fits of tears. Her entire frame visibly convulsed.

Shelby stepped forward either to defend herself or to console Kimber. Garridan wasn't sure, but he held her back. This was his problem, his past, and he wasn't going to drag her into this mess. Not on her birthday, not ever. Kimber needed to know her place. He walked up to her to set things straight once and for all.

"We're over, Kimber." Garridan fought hard to be gentle through his impatience. "We have been for a long time and I'm not sure that what you feel for me is love, but whatever it is, I don't feel that way about you. Shelby is a good woman and I love her. Hopefully she'll say yes and you'll have to make peace with our relationship." He didn't bother correcting her assumption about his proposal.

A sound of disgust bubbled in Kimber's throat and without warning, she slapped Garridan hard across his face. "I hate you!" she screamed, her arms flailing wildly as she tried to hit him again.

Garridan grabbed her wrists but she kicked him in the shin, causing him to double over with a grunt.

"I *hate* you!" This time, she lunged at Shelby, but Quincy and Marc intercepted and carried Kimber across the room.

Not intimidated, Shelby stood in front of Kimber and said, "You're going to get sick. You have to think about the baby."

"Don't talk to me!" she yelled and spat at Shelby, globs of saliva hitting her square in the face.

Seething, Garridan watched as Shelby dragged the sleeve of her sweater over her face, mopping the moisture that was now slowly trickling down her cheek. He jerked Shelby out of Kimber's reach and stood between them.

Facing Kimber, he said, "Don't you *ever* disrespect Shelby like that again!" Anger surged through his veins. His resolve was waning. "I want you out of my house and out of my life. For good. I don't care anymore what you do with yourself. Be self-destructive, ruin your life. I don't care. I just want you gone! Now, Kimber!" He pointed towards the door.

Kimber stepped forward and was so close to Garridan, he could feel her breath on his face. There was a demonic glint in her bloodshot green eyes. He stepped back. He wanted nothing less than to share his personal space with her.

"Get this straight, Garridan," she said in a low, menacing voice. "If you *ever* think about choosing that bitch over me, you'll live to regret it."

She smirked as if she knew the secrets of the universe. When she lunged at him again, Marc jumped between them and clasped her wrists.

Garridan shook his head furiously. "I can't do this," he said running his hands through his hair. "I can't be here right now." He kissed Shelby on her forehead and turned to Marc. "Get her out of here." He pointed at Kimber without looking at her, "I can't be around this woman. I'll be back later."

"I'll go with you," Shelby said, holding onto his arm.

She looked calm but Garridan could hear the concern in her voice.

Kimber sniggered.

"No, baby," he said to Shelby as he held her tightly and kissed the top of her head. "Stay with Megan and Alyssa. The guys will take Kimber home and I'll see you when she's gone, okay?" He gave her one more kiss and turned to leave.

It was a jarring scene to watch. As she sank onto the couch next to Alyssa, Shelby couldn't believe what had just happened. She'd never experienced anything like that and felt as though she was stuck in a soap opera.

"Let go of me!" Kimber yelled as she wrestled out of Marc's grasp. "Don't ever touch me again!"

"Back off, Kimber!" Megan said, standing protectively next to Marc. "Don't even think about slapping Marc or you'll have to deal with me."

Kimber huffed. "Whatever. I'm getting out of here." She sneered at Shelby as she stomped towards the door and said, "If I can't have him, no one will!"

"Kimber, wait! I'll drive y–" Quincy called after Kimber but the door slammed before he could finish.

Everyone breathed a sigh of relief.

"That was intense," Marc said. "Are you okay?" he asked Shelby.

She nodded. "I'm fine, thanks. Will *she* be okay? Should she even be driving?" Shelby worried. Kimber was unstable and shouldn't have been driving at all, much less in the wet weather.

"She'll be fine," Megan said dismissively.

Shelby wasn't convinced. "What did she mean when she said if she can't have him, no one will? I really don't like that."

"It's Kimber. Who knows what's going on inside her

head? This is what she always does," Quincy offered and the others laughed.

Shelby couldn't help being concerned. Kimber's actions weren't normal. She was crying out for help but everyone treated it is if it was just her being her. She needed guidance, advice, a friend. Why was she even out this late? Did she really have no one in her life who cared about her? Shelby couldn't imagine being that alone. She recalled being pregnant with her children and how her family and friends doted on her and made sure she was okay all the time. She doubted any of them would have allowed her to be out alone late at night, driving in the rain.

Sadness for Kimber gripped Shelby's heart and a slow pound started forming in the back of her head. She went to the bathroom to wash her face. She could still smell Kimber's saliva on her.

"Does anyone know where Garridan keeps his painkillers?" she asked when she returned to the living room.

Alyssa stood. "Follow me," she said with a kind smile.

In the kitchen, Alyssa opened a small cabinet above the microwave and handed Shelby a container with tablets.

"It's going to be okay, Shelby," Alyssa said as she gave her a bottle of water from the fridge.

Shelby smiled self-consciously. "I'm not used to this much drama. Is it always like this?"

Alyssa moved her head side to side as if weighing her answer. "Mostly when Kimber is involved. But the rest of the time, things are usually pretty normal. Quiet. Peaceful."

"Why does Garridan allow it? I thought there was a re-straining order against her." Shelby needed to make sense of it all, especially since Garridan wanted her to stay.

"Garridan's compassion is like a curse. It confuses Kimber because, although he says it's over between them, he doesn't completely reject her. No one's ever been as kind or patient with her as Garridan has. We all know it's because of the baby, but she believes it's because of *her*. So, she takes advantage of his good nature and uses every opportunity to get under his skin. She forces herself on him. But as much as it infuriates him, he won't allow her to sit in a cell in her condition."

Shelby nodded. Alyssa was right. Garridan would take the punches before he hurts anyone, especially a woman. But where did he draw the line?

"It's a lot to consider. I don't know how to feel about it. Or what to do," Shelby confessed. For some reason, she trusted Alyssa with this information.

"Garridan loves you, Shelby. We've known him since college and we're all really close. None of us has ever seen him this taken by anyone." Alyssa's tone was filled with love for her friend. "I know you have reservations about staying with him because of what you've seen, but please don't let Kimber's actions rob you and Garridan of the love you clearly feel for each other. Don't allow Kimber to come between you." Alyssa gently patted Shelby's shoulder and left to join the others in the living room.

Shelby stayed in the kitchen for a long time. She thought about Garridan – how long she'd wished for him, how easy it was to love him, how amazing he made her feel and how deep their love was. She also thought about Kimber and all her issues. Would it eventually come to an end?

She'd received advice from Harlow and Alyssa, outside perspectives from both sides. What was she going to do? Garridan's proposal was an offer of a lifetime. The thought of something new excited her – a challenging, yet thrilling new job, and being with Garridan permanently. She would love him coming home to her after a long day or long months of filming. Everything she'd ever wanted and prayed for was right there within her reach, all she had to do was say yes. But, Kimber…

"Shelby!" Megan ran into the kitchen and yanked her from the chair. "Hurry!" she said, dragging Shelby behind her.

When they entered the living room, the tension in the air was thick. Alyssa sat against Quincy on the couch, and Shelby noticed how tightly they held each other's hands. Fear lined their features. They were watching Marc who was pacing the room, holding a cellphone to his ear. Megan squeezed Shelby's hand. What was going on? Marc's words were rushed as he spoke on the phone but in her daze, Shelby couldn't make out what he was saying.

"Which channel?" he asked suddenly. He waited for an answer and cut the call abruptly before grabbing the remote control and turning on the TV.

The words *BREAKING NEWS* stretched across the top of the screen. A reporter was in the shot, an umbrella shielding him against the steady drizzle. Behind him, the lights of emergency vehicles flashed round and around at what looked like an accident scene. Yellow tape created a barrier against the sea of spectators.

Marc turned up the volume.

"...Allyn, reportedly almost full term with her first child, was airlifted a few minutes ago. Her condition remains uncertain," the reporter said.

A collective gasp resonated through the room as they recognised Kimber's surname. Shelby's heart raced as the camera shot zoomed in on the scene. The crew was working hard at a wrecked vehicle crushed between an SUV and a street lamp, its very distinctive tail lights visible in the darkness of the night under the faint glow of the lamp. Garridan's Mustang. Ice instantly coursed through Shelby as the terror she recognised in the others' expressions earlier, now gripped her.

"Emergency personnel are using Jaws of Life in an attempt to extract Luca from his vehicle..." the reporter continued.

Megan's arm flew around Shelby's shoulders and they clung to each other, their bodies vibrating as one. Shelby's knees buckled the moment a pair of strong arms embraced her and Megan from behind. She was certain she'd collapse if it weren't for the support of those arms around her.

"Come," Marc said as he walked them to the couch. "Sit down here."

Shelby realised she'd tethered herself to Megan. She couldn't let go and she couldn't apologise. Her eyes were glued to the TV.

"Please, please, please let him be okay," she whispered

in quiet prayer. Tears blurred her vision but she pinched them away. She had to watch. "Please let him be okay."

On screen, the emergency crew shouted, waved and signalled at others out of the shot. Seconds later, a stretcher was brought towards them. Shelby's heart pounded in her chest as she watched them turn and twist, shouting orders at each other. And finally, they carried Garridan away to the ambulance. His face was swollen and covered in blood, his neck was held steady in a brace and a shiny foil-like blanket was placed over him. He appeared to be unconscious. Fear clutched Shelby's heart and hot tears rolled down her cheeks. It couldn't possibly be real.

The shot zoomed out and focused in on the reporter. "As you can see, emergency services were successfully able to extract Garridan Luca from the wreckage and are transporting him to hospital." The ambulance sirens wailed in the background. "Police are interviewing eyewitnesses to put together the events that led to this horrendous accident..."

Shelby commanded her frozen body into action. The rush of the ambulance and the sirens that echoed in her head gave her hope. She wiped the tears with the heel of her hand, breathed deeply and squared her shoulders. Garridan needed her strong. She had to be strong for his sake. He'll be okay, she thought. He had to be.

She stood. "Can you take me to the hospital, please?" she asked Quincy.

"Yeah, we're all going."

He grabbed his keys and Marc did the same.

Shelby cradled the baby boy to her chest. He was swaddled in a cosy, fluffy blanket she managed to find in the hospital's gift shop. The nurses had exchanged the uncomfortable visitor's chair in Garridan's room for a beautiful and comfortable rocking chair that was usually kept in the nursery.

She rocked back and forth, humming a lullaby while stroking his soft, dark hair. He wriggled slightly and she looked down at him. He was beautiful. His little lips puckered and his mouth moved as if he was sucking on something. Shelby smiled. He was the most precious thing on Earth.

Her heart sank as she thought about his mother. How sad that Kimber had carried him all those months but didn't even get to see him. As troublesome as Kimber was, Shelby never wished her any harm. Her heart ached with sadness when she thought about the painful and tragic way Kimber had died. The baby sniffled and hiccoughed as if he was sorrowful too. Shelby resumed her humming and patted him ever so gently to console him.

"I'm so sorry, little one." She kissed his little forehead and looked down at him again, "I'm sorry, Jamie."

It'd been two days since the accident and Garridan was still unconscious. His doctors were concerned about the slight swelling on his brain and kept him sedated. But when they ran follow-up scans earlier, they gave a more positive prognosis. The worst was over and the swelling had subsided significantly, so they eased him off the sedatives and hoped he'd soon regain consciousness.

Shelby never left his side. It was against hospital regulations but Quincy pulled some strings. As far as the hospital staff was concerned, Shelby was Garridan's fiancée and Jamie was his child. Since his mother had died and his father was unconscious, Shelby was practically the only family the little one had and the only one who should be with him until he was discharged. And just like that, she was allowed to stay.

At night, she slept in a rickety, fold-up bed the hospital grudgingly provided, she showered in the adjoining little bathroom, and ate in the cafeteria downstairs when Jamie was taken to the nursery. She didn't need much. As long as she was close to both of them, she was happy.

She held Garridan's bandaged hand. He lay so still in his bed that the only sign of him being alive was the warmth of his skin and the beeping of the monitors around him. Thankfully, there was only one drip now and the colour in his cheeks was slowly returning. Other than the swelling on the left side of his face where he probably slammed into the door during the collision, and the cuts that speckled his handsome face, he looked much better than he did when they first brought him in. Hopefully, the scars will disappear completely over time.

"I'm here, Garridan," she said as she gently stroked his fingers, careful not to hurt him. "Please get better. I need you with me."

At visiting hours, she left the room to give his family and friends time with him. She stood outside to get some fresh air and visited the nursery. She wondered what Garridan would decide about Jamie. She'd grown to love the little boy and, apart from the nurses, she was the only one he knew. What if the DNA results proved he wasn't Garridan's? Her heart clenched at the thought of him going to live with another family – with a father who didn't even care about him or his mother while she carried him. What kind of life would Jamie have then? Shelby prayed that by some miracle, Jamie would stay with them. She already knew Garridan would want that too.

"Are you alright?" a woman asked from behind Shelby while she watched Jamie through the nursery window.

Recognising Garridan's mother's voice, she turned and said, "Yes, thank you. Are you?"

She'd met Garridan's relatives the night he was rushed in. They talked for a while and she learnt that Garridan had spoken to his mother about her.

"I'm fine now that I know he's out of the woods. I just wanted to thank you for staying with him." Her beautiful eyes looked so much like Garridan's.

"You don't have to thank me," Shelby smiled. "There's nowhere I'd rather be."

Garridan's mother smiled and stood closer to look through the window. "What do you think he'll do about the baby?" she asked.

Shelby didn't have to think about it when she said, "The right thing."

Bright lights stung Garridan's eyes and he shut them immediately. He lay quietly, still, waiting for the dull throb in his head to die off. The loud beeping wasn't helping.

When he opened his eyes again, pain coursed through the left side of his face. He didn't have to touch it to know it was swollen, so he peeked through his right eye and noticed the drip hovering above him. Lifting his head slowly, he ignored the ache that registered through his entire body. Shelby was sitting in a rocking chair beside the bed. She smiled down at a blue bundle cradled in her arms. So beautiful, he thought.

"Did I miss something?" he asked. His throat was scratchy. Dry.

Shelby jerked at the sound of his voice. With wide eyes, she stood slowly and walked towards him still carrying the bundle. A baby.

"Whose baby is that?" he croaked.

After she gently laid the baby down in the cot next to his bed, Shelby held a cup with a straw to Garridan's mouth. He took a sip of the cool water and it immediately soothed his throat. Her eyes were teary and she tried to smile through her emotions. Seeing her like that tugged at his heart. He tried to reach out to her but pain shot through his arm.

"Don't move," she warned. "It's broken. So are your ribs," she added sadly.

He finally looked down at himself. The beeping on the monitor increased in time with his spiking heartbeat. What the hell? His left arm was in a full cast from his shoulder down to his wrist. Bandage covered his torso, as well as his right wrist and hand. His right leg was also in a full cast and elevated on a pillow. He looked at Shelby for answers.

"I'm so glad you're okay." She leaned in, kissing him gently on his temple. He winced.

"What happened?" The last thing he remembered was driving from his house, fleeing one of Kimber's tantrums.

"I think we should call a nurse," she said with a frown.

"No, not yet. I want to know what happened," he insisted.

A look of sadness crossed her face again. "There was an accident," she said. "What do you remember?"

He nodded slowly. "I remember leaving when Kimber spat at you. I'm sorry about that. I was just so angry; I didn't want to do anything rash." He closed his eyes, trying to recall the night. "It was still drizzling and the roads were wet. I was driving through a small neighbourhood close to the freeway and some idiot tailgated me. His high-beams blinded me when I looked into the mirrors. He could easily have overtaken me but I decided to switch lanes and allow him to pass. But as soon as I did, he switched too. The road was empty, so I don't know why he was being such an ass. Next thing I know, he rammed into me. And the rest is a blank." When Shelby sighed and shook her head, he asked, "What is it?"

She told him about Kimber's threat after he left, about her storming out of the house, and how they watched scenes on TV of the accident that caused his injuries, claimed Kimber's life, and brought a baby into the world.

"What are you telling me, babe?" His voice felt strained.

She closed her eyes and inhaled deeply as if she was drawing strength from an unseen source. "It wasn't *some idiot*, Garridan. It was Kimber. Witnesses said that when she rammed into you, you lost control and collided head on with the street lamp and you were flung halfway through the windshield," she rattled off.

"What else?" he asked.

"Kimber didn't stop there. As you said, the road was empty, so she reversed her car and rammed into you two more times at high speed. Evidence indicates that her airbag deployed the first time, and the second time, the impact caused the steering wheel to crush her against the seat. That's when she finally stopped. She suffered multiple broken bones and profuse internal bleeding.

"You were spared because of the Mustang's sturdiness. The top half of your body was splayed across your car's bonnet and your legs were pinned on the inside. The rescue team had to use Jaws of Life to free you from the crushed metal that encased you. Doctors say you're lucky to be alive," she squeaked out the last sentence.

Garridan gasped as the images Shelby created reeled in his mind. "What about Kimber? And the baby?" he asked.

"Kimber was conscious when they airlifted her but died

on the way to the hospital. Paramedics had to deliver the baby in the helicopter." She picked the baby up and kissed its head. "Thankfully, he was okay. He's perfect."

Garridan looked at the baby in her arms. He didn't know how to feel. Kimber tried to kill him. How did a simple and brief romance lead to this much devastation? It was too much to process. A searing pain issued through his head and he groaned loudly as he pinched his eyes closed, bracing himself against it. The beeping and buzzing of the machines intensified as the pain caused him to shudder. He gritted his teeth. It felt as though his head would explode at any second.

"I'm calling the nurse," Shelby said.

Shelby smiled up at Garridan as she sat beside his bed feeding the baby. She looked so at ease and it tugged at his heart to see her so content.

"For someone who didn't want more kids, you look awfully happy," he teased.

She giggled softly. "I am. Who can resist this precious little face?" she said in a sing-song voice as she looked down at the baby.

Garridan smiled, knowing exactly what she meant. After his meltdown the day before, the doctors examined him and administered strong painkillers which made him a little more agreeable. He spent some time with Shelby and the baby, and had to admit the little one had stolen his heart too.

"Do you still want to do the DNA test?" Shelby asked, pulling him out of his reverie.

He'd already thought about it. "No," he replied honestly. "I don't need a test to prove he deserves to grow up loved and protected. I want to be the one to give him that."

Shelby bit her bottom lip and smiled, obviously pleased with his decision. "He deserves everything good this world has to offer," she said.

Garridan thought about Kimber. He wondered if motherhood would've changed her. What kind of mother would she have been? He didn't always get along with her, especially towards the end, but he never intended for things to turn out this badly. As peaceful as that moment with Shelby and the baby was, it still wasn't right that Kimber had died. He wondered how and when he'd tell the baby about his mother and why she wasn't with him anymore. The thought alone was too much to bear. He decided to cross that bridge when the time was right.

"Do you want to name him?" he asked Shelby who seemed lost in thoughts of her own.

She smiled shyly.

Garridan cocked an eyebrow. "You already named him, didn't you?"

"I couldn't keep calling him *the baby*," she scoffed, rolling her eyes.

"I just realised I was doing the same thing," he laughed. "Okay, what's his name?"

"I call him Jamie. For James." She looked at him curiously.

He liked it. "Why James?"

"Because of Jameson – the character that brought you to yourself. When life began," she said as a matter of fact.

He recalled their conversation about his life as an actor, and how he felt about certain roles. His heart swelled knowing that Shelby took one life-altering experience and incorporated it with another.

"James Luca," he said with appreciation. "James Sheldon Luca."

"Sheldon?" Shelby frowned.

"Named for you," he answered her unasked question. "Unless you can think of something more suitable."

She shook her head. "Sheldon is perfect. Thank you."

"I should be thanking *you*. I don't know what I would've done without you." He reached out and she placed her hand in his. "I love you."

"I love you too, Garridan," her voice trembled. "I'm so grateful all my prayers were answered."

"You know, you never did answer my question." Garridan couldn't believe it'd been just four days since he asked Shelby to stay with him. So much had happened that it felt like ages ago.

"Yes, Garridan," she said without hesitation. "I'll always say yes to you."

He raised his eyebrows. "Is that so?" he asked. "Then will you answer one more question?"

"Of course," she shrugged.

Garridan caressed her fingers with his thumb. He wished he could've done it differently. He'd promised to take things slow, but he wasn't wasting any more time. Life was too short to wait for the perfect moment. He almost didn't make it to see this day. He was spared, saved from certain death and he was blessed to be holding the hand of the most incredible woman he'd ever known, who was cradling the most beautiful baby boy he'd ever seen. He wasn't going to wait any longer to start living his life. This was the beginning of their life together.

"Babe," he said, swallowing hard. His voice felt thick with emotion and tears welled in his eyes. "You know you're everything to me." Shelby nodded and he continued, "No one loves me the way you do, and there are no words in any language strong enough to express how deeply I love you. My life is meaningless without you. I don't ever want us to be apart again." His voice broke as he finally gave in to his emotions and allowed the tears to fall. "Will you marry me?"

Garridan watched as first shock then elation registered on Shelby's features. Tears she couldn't contain streaked her cheeks. She closed her fingers around his and laughed through her sobs before she replied.

"Yes," she cried. "I'll marry you."

EPILOGUE

Los Angeles, United States of America
One year later

"Where would you like me to put these?" Harlow asked, looking up at the bunch of balloons floating above her head.

"You're the party planner," Shelby said. "I trust your instincts."

Harlow rubbed her cute little bump as she waddled across the room. She tied the balloons to a single chair next to a giant plastic letter J that stood in a corner where the gifts had started piling up.

"Thank you for doing this," Shelby said as she joined Harlow who took one last look around the room.

"You don't have to thank me. There's nothing I won't do for that boy. He is my godson after all."

"Your hands will soon be full with your own little bundle of joy," Shelby said as she absently stroked Harlow's protruding belly.

"Four more months. I'm so excited, I really can't wait."

"I'm so happy for you, Harlow. You're going to be such a great mom," Shelby said, enveloping her cousin in an embrace.

"Thank you, Shel. I appreciate that and I appreciate you," she said before she excused herself to check on the caterers.

A party for Jamie's first birthday was something Shelby and Garridan had debated. His view was that Jamie was too young to understand its significance, while she felt that a first birthday was a milestone that simply had to be celebrated. She won. And she was glad because Harlow did a beautiful job decorating the room using Jamie's current obsession as the theme.

The main table was set up in front of a large Styrofoam train cut-out that occupied most of the back wall. It was pleasantly decorated with colourful, spiralled streamers, a two-tier train-themed cake, platters of savoury finger foods, and bowls of assorted sweets and potato chips. Pictures of different types of trains hung from the ceiling and walls. Several tiny wooden tables and chairs were placed strategically in the spacious room, where the twins and Daniel had assembled a train set to run between them.

Shelby stood back and looked around the room. Her heart swelled. For the first time in over a year, everyone she loved would soon arrive to be in the same place at the same time to celebrate Jamie's special day. It had been a year of ups and downs and she was relieved and thankful for some normality. Looking back, she couldn't believe everything they'd been through.

As soon as Garridan was doing better after the accident, Jamie was discharged from the hospital and Shelby brought him home. The blissful moment was overshadowed by the fact that there wasn't a room or clothes or anything else to welcome home their baby boy, and although the sudden arrival of a new born in their lives couldn't have been anticipated, Garridan felt terrible about not being prepared. He asked Shelby to prepare a room and to fill it with everything Jamie would ever need. Shelby enlisted Megan's help and in no time, Jamie had a beautiful room and everything that went with it to call his own.

Garridan was hospitalised for a few weeks, and it took several months for him to properly recover from his injuries. He also had to attend intense physiotherapy sessions to assist with muscle and joint recuperation. Thankfully, the filming that was supposed to commence in the March following the accident, was postponed until he was back to full health. He enjoyed a few weeks at home with Shelby and Jamie before travelling to Atlanta where he spent four months working.

In between, Shelby helped Harlow plan for her big day, attended their beautiful wedding in Miami, and returned to Johannesburg to arrange for her relocation to L.A. Fortunately, Garridan had access to resources that fast tracked the application process, and everything came together seamlessly. She was amazed at how everyone in both her and Garridan's lives rallied around to support them and help out wherever they could.

Their own wedding, although a first for both of them, was an intimate affair in the privacy of their home. It was a small gathering but Garridan and Shelby wanted it to be special and memorable. And it was. The ceremony took place in the garden. Shelby wore a simple but chic off-white satin dress and Garridan looked dashing in a classic black suit. Their four sons made up their bridal party. They wrote their own vows which were choked out through sobs of happy tears in the presence of a handful of family and close friends. They forewent a honeymoon and requested donations instead of gifts. What they received, as well as what they would've spent on the honeymoon, were used to establish an outreach organisation for pregnant women who had no support and those suffering with depression.

Of course, like everything else in life, bitter accompanied the sweet. When news about Kimber's tragic death surfaced, the internet went crazy. The public was mostly sympathetic and supportive of Garridan and Shelby, but despite the facts being reported in the media, Kimber's followers were unrelenting, blaming Garridan's apparent infidelity for her death and accusing Shelby of wrecking their happy home. Although they knew it wasn't true, the perception of what had happened caused feelings of guilt. Garridan and Shelby relied heavily on each other during those trying times and instead of tearing them apart, the ordeal strengthened their bond. They'd long ago planned to set the record straight regarding Kimber's connection to Garridan, but in light of her death, they agreed not to. Eventually, the publicity surrounding the incident tapered off and the cyber-battering came to an end.

As the months passed, thanks to Garridan's guidance, Shelby learnt to deal with the attention from the public and gradually, it also became a part of her everyday life.

Regardless of everything they'd endured, Shelby loved her amazing and full life. She had everything she'd ever wanted, everything she'd ever needed, and would be forever grateful for every single event that laid the path that brought her to that very moment. She closed her eyes and sent up a quick prayer of thanks.

"There she is," Garridan said in a sing-song voice behind her.

Shelby turned and her heart pinched as Garridan, with Jamie in his arms, joined her in the room. No matter how many times she saw it, her heart still fluttered, her stomach still flipped and her knees still got weak. There was nothing more attractive to her than seeing her incredible husband carry their beautiful son in his arms.

"Hi, you two," she said, mimicking his sing-song voice for the sake of Jamie who beamed when he saw her, showing off his four little pearly white teeth.

"What are you doing, birthday girl?" Garridan asked, holding out his free arm.

She stepped into his sideways embrace and folded her arms around his waist. "Just doing final checks."

"It looks great," he said, nodding as he surveyed the room.

"Mama," Jamie murmured. He tipped forward and held his arms out towards Shelby.

"Come to Mama, birthday boy," she said.

He clambered into her arms and when she tickled his belly, he threw his head back and chuckled. His green eyes sparkled brightly. He was such a happy baby. Shelby loved being a mom to a little one again and Garridan was an amazing dad. Together, they were wonderful parents. Jamie was steeped in love and lacked for absolutely nothing.

"Some of the guests have arrived, babe," Garridan said, pulling her back into his side as Jamie settled on her hip.

"Okay," she said, looking up at him. "Thank you for today."

"Anything to make you happy," he said. He leaned down and planted sweet, gentle kisses on her lips. "I love you."

"I love you too," she said, pinching her thigh. Sometimes she still couldn't believe he was hers and that this was her life.

"Ready?" he asked softly, threading her fingers with his.

"Yes," she smiled.

And hand in hand they left to welcome their guests.